DEBORAH MALONE

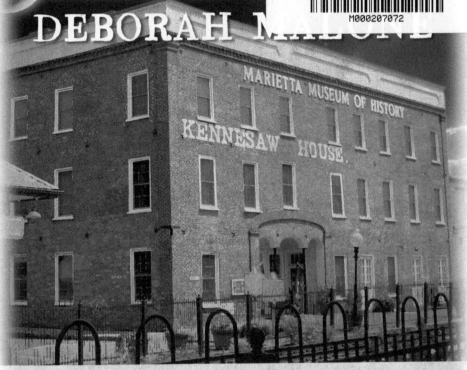

MURDER IN MARIETTA

A TRIXIE MONTGOMERY COZY MYSTERY

A LAMP POST BOOK

MURDER IN MARIETTA
BY DEBORAH MALONE

ISBN 10: 1-60039-199-0
ISBN 13: 978-1-60039-199-6
ebook ISBN: 978-1-60039-724-0

www.lamppostpubs.com

MURDER IN MARIETTA

a Trixie Montgomery cozy mystery

BY DEBORAH MALONE

Deborah Malone

MURDER IN MARIETTA

a Trixie Montgomery cozy mystery

BY DEBORAH MALONE

Deborah Malone

Be kind and compassionate to one another, forgiving each other, just as in Christ, God forgave you.

Ephesians 4:32 (NIV)

ACKNOWLEDGEMENTS

I would like to thank the director of the Marietta Museum of History, Dan Cox and his lovely wife, Connie for all their help with research on the museum.

Thanks go to all of the readers of *Death in Dahlonega* who have encouraged me to continue writing about Trixie, Dee Dee, and Nana. To all the book clubs who invited me to come share my writing journey and have invited me back for "Murder in Marietta."

A special thank you goes to Beverly Nault for editing "Murder in Marietta." Trixie and Dee Dee thank you, too.

Dedication

Murder in Marietta is dedicated to my family and friends
who continue to encourage me.

A special dedication to my readers – you keep me writing.

CHAPTER ONE

Marietta, Georgia

I flipped over a fresh page in my reporter's notebook as my best friend, Dee Dee, dug into the most enormous slice of Chocolate Fetish mocha pie I'd ever seen. Dee Dee smacking loudly, I fought to keep a journalist's objectivity while Doc Pennington, the director of the Marietta History Museum, recounted the most recent ghost sightings.

"Doc, what I really want to know is…" My tummy roiled considering the possibilities. "Have you personally seen the resident phantom?" All at once I hoped he'd say no, but from the excitement that grew in his expression, I knew he was about to confirm my worst fears.

"As a matter of fact, Trixie, may I call you Trixie?"

I nodded and he went on.

"Shortly after I became director of the museum, I heard rumors of ghosts. Until recently I didn't give them any real credence. Not until unexplainable occurrences happened." He waited while a young man refilled our tea glasses.

"Such as?" My voice quavered as I prompted Doc, once the waiter was out of earshot.

"Like when the door on the empty elevator opened and closed." Doc rubbed the bridge of his nose underneath horn-rimmed bifocals. "Once I saw a lady adorned in period clothes from the Civil War Era. Another time a man dressed in uniform appeared. I thought I'd been around this history stuff too long and my imagination ran wild."

I glanced at Dee Dee, my memories transporting me to a time when one of the neighborhood kids wore a sheet and jumped out at me in the inky darkness. I've never forgotten the feeling of my heart skipping a few beats. It was a long time before the kids stopped laughing about the embarrassing stain that spread across my corduroys. Since that fateful night the mention of ghosts stirs a cauldron of ugly feelings. When Harv, my editor at "Georgia by the Way," gave me this assignment, I knew I'd have to deal with unresolved childhood fears. Until Doc began recounting the sightings, I didn't realize how close to the surface they would rise.

I'd been at the magazine for less than a year, and trying to prove myself among the younger, more energetic reporters. So when Harv suggested I spend a night at the museum, I said yes. Doc was a good friend of Harv's and had made the arrangements, so I couldn't afford to mess things up with my unreasonable fears. I forced my thoughts back to the present as Doc continued.

"I decided to have a little fun and talk up the sightings. Word spread faster than a pat of butter on a hot biscuit. People flocked to the museum to meet the ghosts. PBS, TBS, CBS, TNN and "Haunted House" on the History Channel featured the story. The tale literally took on a life of its own as everyone tried to see a ghost. But when no one showed, they all said I was trying to get publicity."

"Or that he was crazy," Penny, his wife, hissed, patting his hand. "We were practically ostracized from the community. For a while they stopped bringing in school children for tours."

"I understand why Harv wants to scoop with the big guys. I just wish he hadn't asked me to jump in with him." I've heard you can smell fear. I certainly hoped that wasn't true in the case of ghosts.

"Honey." Penny laid her hand on Doc's arm, "tell them what's happened lately." The efficient waiter returned, cleared the table and refilled our tea glasses. Doc took his time as if weighing his next words.

"A few weeks ago, a couple of things happened that weren't so benign. Before those incidents, most of the episodes were explainable. You know, malfunctioning elevator, creaky sounds emitted from an old building. Then the events changed."

"Like what?" I took a long sip of cold sweet tea and swiped at my mouth with the cloth napkin. I was grateful my hand wasn't as shaky as my nerves.

"We arrived one morning to find furniture rearranged in some of the displays. Another night, when I was working late, I smelled smoke. I followed the scent, and discovered a small trashcan on fire. I was alone in the museum, and it was after hours. We have a system that must be armed and disarmed when you enter or leave the lobby."

"I set the alarm before I left," his wife added.

"No one could arrive without me knowing."

"The fire was bad enough, but artifacts began to disappear," Penny said. "Gloria Hamilton's purse was stolen. She's one of our board members, and she jumped at the chance to use this occasion to make Doc look incompetent. She has her radar set on him."

Her chin quivered, and I yearned to give her a hug. "Penny, it's obvious why these events have you upset." I laid a hand on the woman's trembling arm. "What do you think is going on, Doc?"

"Beats me." He rubbed his forehead. "I didn't believe in ghosts before these incidents happened. Now, I'm not so sure. I haven't figured out how a person entered without setting off the buzzer."

The more Doc talked, the more I reconsidered job security. Was my bank balance worth risking a night in a crypt?

"During our discussions, Harv said he wanted you to stay overnight at the museum in hopes you'd encounter a ghost. It's understandable if you choose not to spend the night." Doc hesitated for a moment. "I wanted you to have the facts before you made your decision. I couldn't live with myself if the uninvited visitors played havoc while you were there."

"If your answer's yes," he went on, "Penny and I will be happy to set up a place to sleep. We'll teach you to batten down the hatches before we leave."

My stomach churned, but I played it cool. I knew if I revealed my fear, Dee Dee wouldn't stay and I needed her support. No way was I going to stay in the museum by myself. "Harv's expecting me to hang out with the ethereal residents, so I don't expect I have a choice in the matter. Maybe we'll discover a logical explanation for these strange occurrences. Coincidence, perhaps?" I looked around the table for confirmation. Silence.

"I'm warning you, Trix." Dee Dee pointed her finger in my direction. "This is something we don't need to get mixed up in." She emitted a most un-lady like burp. "Excuse me," she said as she covered her mouth with her napkin – a little late.

"Harv's given me a job to accomplish, and as a reporter I must do my duty," I said bravely, not mentioning the urgency added by the stack of unpaid bills on my kitchen counter at home.

"Oh, please, bury the martyr. You know you can't resist an adventure." Dee Dee's observation touched closer to the truth than I wanted to admit, but I had her duped for now. I'd never shared my childhood experience and the underlying fears it had embedded deep within. I continued with the farce.

"Well, it's a good thing I decided to follow through with our little *adventure* we experienced in Dahlonega." This past fall, Dee Dee had tagged along while I worked on an assignment about Gold Rush Days. During our stay she became a person of interest in a murder case. I had no intention of letting my best friend in the whole world take the rap for a homicide she didn't commit.

We decided to investigate on our own, and before the case was over we helped nab the real killers. But not before I injured my bad knee. The damaged joint required surgery, and now I walk with a little limp. I still need my cane for long treks. The surgeon explained a total replacement awaited me in the near future. More bills.

I looked across the table at Dee Dee, rubbed the offending joint, and emitted an awful groan, akin to a woman in labor.

"You win!" Dee Dee acquiesced. She donned a bemused smile.

With bellies full, we strolled back to the museum. I played the hurt knee card and walked slower than necessary, in hopes of postponing the inevitable. Doc and Penny helped us take our bags inside and showed us several available rooms we might choose to settle down in for the night.

The elevator opened into the lobby, directly in front of the visitor's desk. A stained-glass sign above the desk was etched with the word "Marietta" in red. The dimly lit room and the musty smell of the old museum elicited thoughts of a ghost filled building. It didn't help put me at ease.

To the right of the elevator a little gift shop overflowed with historic books and memorabilia. The first room Doc showed us was the Andrews' Raider's room. This room contained artifacts from the Civil War, also referred to as the War Between the States by southerners. He explained that James Andrews was a northern spy who stole the General, one of the South's trains. The incident was referred to as The Great Locomotive Chase. The whole gang was eventually caught, and Andrews was hanged. I'd heard the story before, but enjoyed listening to Doc's interpretation. Dee Dee and I eyed each other, and silently agreed this was not the room we wanted to sleep in.

We continued the tour through the music area, the fifties-era kitchen, and the quilt room. We chose the quilt room, with its beautiful creations hung on racks along the wall. Cozy and reassuring.

Doc showed us how to operate the security system, then he and Penny bade us goodbye. Dee Dee, her face a shade paler than a white camellia, stalled the couple by asking them numerous benign questions. I didn't blame her. When they left, we'd be alone. Well, except for any nighttime visitors.

While we set up our make shift camp, I studied the quilts. I couldn't even appreciate the tiny hand stitching in the antique hangings, while I imagined the ghosts of their crafters, peering at me from behind a rack.

Dee Dee, positioned on the floor, pulled out various snacks from her purse, which, more often than not, resembled a small carry on case.

"Come on Dee Dee." I unfolded our sleeping bags and rolled them out. "Doc told us to make ourselves at home in the kitchenette. An expedition will be fun. We can snoop on the way."

Dee Dee wasn't taking the bait, so I threw out another morsel. "Isn't this great? How often in a lifetime do you get a chance to spend the night in a museum and have free rein to roam as you please?" My pep talk wasn't doing much to convince me either.

"Well, never is far too many times for me," Dee Dee said.

"Aw, you're a party pooper. Come on." I grabbed her arm and encouraged her to get up. "You'll agree with me later. When the cows come home, you'll be glad you didn't miss out on the fun."

If Dee Dee only knew the battle that raged in my mind, maybe we could comfort each other. Why couldn't I tell her about the fear that threatened to expose my facade of courage? We had shared so many things over the past year since I had moved back home to be close to Mama and Nana. Why couldn't I share this?

"Yeah, sure." Her enthusiasm was underwhelming.

We snooped around in earnest – or rather I did. Dee Dee stuck to me like a tick on a hound dog.

As we crept down the hallway, I imagined courageous pioneers who had walked before us on the highly polished floors. Artifacts covered the walls. Each chamber was designated a different era or given a certain theme, such as the room where Andrews' Raiders had spent the night. I wondered if the ethereal spirits had dared bother them, and eyed a bayonet.

We hurried back to the cozy quilt room, where Dee Dee proceeded to rummage through her snacks. I eyed them with longing. She laughed, "Now who's your best friend?"

"Why, you, of course." I gave her a big hug. Yes, we joked, but I told the truth. We weren't friends merely because she possessed all the food. Over the past year, after my divorce, no one supported me more than Dee Dee. I've strived to be as supportive in return. Gary, her husband of twenty years, had died of a sudden heart attack less than two years ago.

"I need to go to the bathroom," she said. This used to be a nuisance for her, but I'd finally convinced her to visit her doctor. Now, like the leaky pipe ladies in the television ads, Dee Dee wore a patch invented

for those who needed a little extra help. The change was nothing short of a miracle.

"You remember where the restroom is, right? The women's is down the hall and to the left of the elevator."

"If you think I'm going by myself, you're not thinking clearly. No way am I traveling anywhere in this mausoleum without you." She stood and waited for me. "Need a hand?" I raised mine; she grabbed and gave a good pull.

The dim hallway was a little disconcerting. We'd turned on a few lamps along the way, and shadows decorated the walls and floors. I sensed a chill in the air. But only in pockets that seemed to make no sense in relation to the air ducts.

I led the way. Dee Dee followed so close, I felt her hot breath on my neck. We slinked down the hall, through the 1950's kitchen exhibit. Next, we entered the music room. I wouldn't have been surprised if the piano or organ had played anonymously, like in "The Ghost and Mr. Chicken."

I stopped quicker than a Southern girl could say, "*Well, bless her heart.*"

Dee Dee bumped into me. "Trix, what on earth are you doing?"

Mouth flapping open, I couldn't bring myself to tell her about the cool breeze that ruffled my hair and the little shiver of fear that ran down my spine.

CHAPTER TWO

A vent high above the bathroom door was the cool breeze culprit. "Uh, sorry Dee Dee, thought I felt a cool front moving in." I pointed to the airway above the bathroom door. "Let's hurry up and hightail it back to our room."

I didn't linger, brushing my teeth and making sure this was the last time I'd need to visit the facilities until morning.

Safely back in the quilt room, Dee Dee glanced at her watch. "It's still kind of early. What are we going to do now?"

I straightened the pallets. "We could tell ghost stories."

"Very funny," Dee Dee said. "I'm not sure about you, but I don't think I'll be able to sleep a wink. Let's make a pact to keep each other awake just in case we doze off, though."

We chatted like teenage girls for the next couple of hours. Before I knew it, we must have nodded off to sleep, because I awoke with the sense of an unknown presence nearby. I bolted upright! My heart raced so fast, I feared the organ might burst out of my chest. Sweat popped out on my forehead. I sat up, stock still, afraid to breathe. The hair on my arms shot up like porcupine quills. We weren't alone in the room. I made a hair-trigger decision, and shook Dee Dee awake. I wasn't about to face the unknown without company.

"What?" She moaned and shoved at my hand.

"Shhhh." I touched my lips with a finger.

"What? Why did you wake me?" she whispered. Now awake, she sat up. A clammy hand latched onto my arm. I quickly prayed the body part belonged to Dee Dee.

"I don't know. Something woke me up. I have a terrible feeling we're not alone."

"Oh, you're probably dreaming. I'm tired. I'm just going to rest my eyes." She loosened her death grip on my arm and lay back down.

"Look, did you see that?" My stomach tightened, searching the shadowy corners of the room.

"See what?" Dee Dee twisted around.

"Over there, a man dressed in a Union uniform." I must be dreaming. Maybe I was still asleep. "Dee Dee, pinch me," I said. She obliged without a second thought. "Ouch!"

"Why did you holler? You told me to pinch you." Even though darkness hindered my sight, I sensed her big grin.

"Yeah, but you didn't have to enjoy it so much," I whined. "Did you spot him? Quick, help me find my camera." She made no effort to help.

"Trix, quit scaring me. That's not funny." No sooner had the words left her mouth than she was digging her claws into me, for real this time. "I d-d-d-don't see a male ghost – unless he's wearing a skirt."

"What!" My ghost was a soldier; no way he'd be caught dead in a skirt. In a flash, reality hit me like a snowball in winter. Dee Dee didn't see my ghost. She saw another one.

The apparitions were gone as fast as they appeared. "Come on; let's try to make the best of this. After all, I'm here to get a story on Doc's visitors. Right? Why don't you attempt to get some sleep and I'll keep watch. I'm sure they won't come back, now they know we're here. We probably scared them as much as they scared us." *Yeah, right!* When we told Harv we'd seen them as well, he might be a happy camper, but I sure wasn't. I could've lived a lifetime without seeing a ghost. Camera in hand, I twiddled with the settings, wondering which button was best for apparitions.

"I won't be able to sleep a wink. My night is ruined." Dee Dee pulled down her zipper. "I guess it won't kill me to try."

I hope you're right, Dee Dee.

"You promise to stand guard? Just in case?"

"Sure, you can count on me." Famous last words. I wouldn't have to work very hard to keep the ole' peepers open. I knew this story could potentially be a real boost for my career. When Wade, my ex-husband, divorced me for greener pastures, I had to get a job. Twenty years had passed since I'd been in the workforce.

With my confidence about as low as a snake's belly, I applied everywhere, but Harv was the only one willing to give this newbie a chance. The pay wasn't much, but it kept the wolves from the door. Even though my probation period was up, I felt I was still under the microscope. I had to accept every assignment, and make each article a little better than the last. Maybe a Pulitzer awaits me in the future. Way in the future.

As I struggled to stay awake, I pictured the museum piece as a feature article. Next, I imagined all the national magazines and news channels calling me for personal appearances. Last thing I remember, Diane Sawyer was sitting across from me, interviewing 'Moi.' She wore a beige sweater complemented with a dark brown skirt. The prettiest pair of high heels adorned her feet. And to add chocolate on top of the ice cream, guess who sat beside me? None other than Harrison Ford. I'd finally made it. I wondered if Daddy would be proud of me now. Take that, Wade Middlebrooks Montgomery, III.

As Harrison leaned over to give me a big kiss on the cheek - the most dreadful noise erupted that didn't have any place in mine and Harrison's dream. And who in their right mind shook me? How dare they wake me? Didn't they value their life? Dee Dee would pay big time for this. I pried open an eye – it wasn't Dee Dee! An ashen-faced Doc kneeled by my side.

"Doc! What's the matter? Did you see the ghosts?" He made a valiant effort to answer. His mouth moved, but no words came out. He gripped his chest.

"Oh, my goodness. Dee Dee! Wake up. Doc's having a heart attack!"

She went from rustling around, to sitting straight up, in zero to sixty. She climbed over me to reach Doc.

"You give him mouth-to-mouth, and I'll apply chest compressions," Dee Dee commanded as she pushed Doc down on the floor.

Dee Dee's been itching to save someone since she completed her CPR course. It didn't faze her confidence a bit that it took her three times to pass.

"Wait a minute, Dee Dee. Let's check for a pulse first."

"Oh, yeah." She poked around his neck. Doc pushed her hand away. "He's fighting us Trix, he must be in shock. Go ahead with mouth to mouth." Raw fear rose in his eyes as he stammered, grabbing my arm.

"No, no," he sputtered. "I'm not having a heart attack, and I didn't see a ghost."

"Then spit it out, man. What's wrong with you?" Dee Dee's body, coiled, was still prepared to jump on Doc and use compressions if necessary. I laid a hand on her arm to hold her back.

"Come on. I'll show you. It's awful, just awful," he moaned as we scrambled to help him stand. It amazed me how fast his speech came back; I thought he was a goner a moment ago.

We followed him out of the quilt room and down the hall. I held Dee Dee's arm and pulled her along. If I had to witness what was *awful, just awful* she did, too.

We stopped in the doorway of the Andrews' Raiders display. "There," Doc said, pointing.

I pulled Dee Dee forward and peeked inside. Nothing jumped out at me. Then again, a dead body isn't going to jump far. Dee Dee's voice sounded far away as everything went black.

CHAPTER THREE

My eyelids fluttered open. I awoke propped upright on a stark white stretcher, a blood pressure cuff squeezed my arm, and an oxygen mask covered my mouth and nose. A paramedic held a needle, at least six inches long, poised, ready to aim. The young woman appeared way too eager to stick the offending weapon somewhere.

"Don't do that!" I wondered if she understood my muffled cry.

"Hey, Joe! We've got a live one over here," she called to her partner.

"You better believe I'm alive!" I grabbed at the oxygen mask.

"Whoa there ma'am. You've had a bad scare and we need to make sure you're okay. Let's take the pressure one more time before you stand up. We don't want you to drop like a sack of potatoes again." The paramedic squeezed the bulb to tighten the cuff around my arm.

"Hey, Trix." Dee Dee placed her hand on my shoulder. "Relax. You gave us a scare. Let the EMT do her job." Dee Dee looked like she needed to be on the stretcher instead of me. Her face was pale as biscuit dough.

Then I remembered. "Is he...?"

"Yep. Dead as a doornail. Killed with a bayonet." Dee Dee always did have a way with words.

"Who is it? What happened?" I strained to sit up, but my head swirled and I feared I would pass out again. I was amazed at how much strength a body needed to maneuver from lying down to standing up.

"They haven't identified him yet, and they probably wouldn't tell us if they had."

"Let me help you up." The young female EMT removed the blood pressure cuff and the oxygen mask. She grabbed my hand and pulled me to a sitting position. "Sit there until you get your bearings."

I surveyed the room. Doc stood in the corner talking with a couple of uniformed policemen. Two men, their heads close together in conversation, knelt beside the body. One was Joe, the EMT, but I didn't recognize the other one decked out in a nice suit. I wondered if he was the medical examiner.

An unfamiliar man dressed in a rumpled trench coat, reminiscent of Columbo, walked toward me. I pegged him to be in his late fifties or early sixties. His black hair streaked with gray, matched his thick, bushy eyebrows that reminded me of two caterpillars.

His wrinkled suit gave the impression he'd slept in it. A big fat cigar stuck out of his mouth. *Please let him walk past me.*

"Ms. Montgomery?" His rough, craggy voice belied years of smoking. He stabbed an unlit cigar at me. "Are you better?"

"Ugh, I guess I am."

"I'm Detective Bowerman from Marietta P.D. I need to ask you and your friend some questions. One of the officers will stay with you until you're questioned." He turned and walked away.

"Can you get up now?" The young EMT shouted, as if I were deaf.

"Yes, I think I can," I said. She grabbed one arm and Dee Dee clutched the other. Between both of them they stood me up. They held on tightly until I steadied myself.

"Ladies, I'm going to see if the Medical Examiner needs me." She observed me and said, "If you feel faint again, be sure and alert us." She hurried over to assist the M.E.

Dee Dee hung on to me like Stonewall Jackson hung on to Manassas. I welcomed her support. "Dee, did you see the body? He was all crumpled, and there was so much blood."

She nodded. "Yes, I did." She leaned and whispered in my ear, "Not again, Trix. Why us?"

"I don't know." The reason we kept stumbling over dead bodies was a mystery to me.

The officers made their way over and introduced themselves as Officer Debra Roach and Officer Rick Trapp. A nervous laugh escaped my lips. Dee Dee covered her mouth in an attempt to keep from laughing out loud.

"Don't worry, we've heard all the jokes. Follow me ladies," Officer Trapp said. Dee Dee and I walked arm in arm until he announced, "Ms. Lamont, you come with me. Ms. Montgomery can go with Officer Roach."

"Can't we stay together?" Dee Dee pleaded.

"I'm afraid not. Detective Bowerman wants you to remain in separate areas until he speaks with you." Officer Debra wasn't someone you'd want to disagree with. Built like a linebacker, she stood a good six feet tall. Her short spiky hair only increased her macho appearance. So, I gave Dee Dee a forlorn look as we went our separate ways. She answered with a hang-dog expression.

Officer Debra and I passed Doc's office. Detective Bowerman sat on the edge of Doc's desk. Doc squirmed in his chair like a worm on a fishhook. I anticipated my turn as much as a root canal.

CHAPTER FOUR

After Officer Debra and I exchanged niceties, no one spoke. The silence became deafening, and I broke like a tortured woman. "What do you think is keeping them? Why wouldn't they let Dee Dee come with me? It's not like we're in cahoots or anything," I blabbed.

She observed me with pity. "There's no need for concern, Trixie. Detective Bowerman just likes to interview the witnesses separately. Shouldn't be too much longer."

Easy for her to say. I sat in the hot seat waiting to be questioned by a *wanna be* Columbo.

"I hope he hurries. I want to check on Dee Dee and Doc. And I need to call my editor to update him on what's happened."

"Yes, ma'am." She straightened her gun belt and repositioned her pleasantly plump body in her chair.

Time passed slower than a snail riding on a turtle's back. When Detective Bowerman finally entered the room, he glanced at Officer Debra and said, "Officer Roach, help secure the scene." I wanted to shout, *please take me with you. I'm a quick learner and I can help.* But I didn't say a word to her, and she left me alone with Columbo.

"Detective, would you tell me how my friend is doing?" I clasped my hands in silent prayer.

He chewed on his unlit cigar and answered in his own sweet time. "Your friend is fine. She's shook up of course, but you don't have to worry; she's in good hands. And I'll ask the questions now."

Geeze Louise. "All right."

I must have talked on and on, gauging by his glassy-eyed stare by the time I slowed down. I explained the reason we spent the night at the museum and how we met Doc and Penny. Next, I mentioned the mysteries Doc told me had plagued the museum lately.

I described our delicious meal at Hemingway's Bar and Grill, at which point my stomach emitted an unlady-like growl. Of course, I revealed the Chocolate Fetish was to die for, and if he ever had a chance to eat at Hemingway's he needed to sample it. I reckon the only reason he listened to all of the useless details was because he wanted to separate the wheat from the chaff.

I shared how Dee Dee had procured a bee in her bonnet when I told her the assignment required me to spend the night in the museum with the resident ghosts. Amazingly, he didn't stop me then and there. I revealed Harv had sprung this on me, and I wasn't too thrilled about the assignment either. Taking a deep breath, I related how Doc claimed to see the ghosts and how the media ran with the story.

I continued the saga of our harrowing night up to the moment Doc woke me, and that his sickly appearance spurred me to assume he was having a heart attack. Without skipping a beat, I ended with the big finale – when Doc showed us the body and everything went blank. I sat back in my chair and let out a sigh.

"Are you finished, Ms. Montgomery?" Bowerman stared at me.

I wanted to say, *well duh.* The truth – the fight in me had been extinguished, so I politely answered, "Yes, sir." I felt the perspiration dripping down my forehead. I guess the detective noticed, too. He offered me some Kleenex and I gently wiped the droplets away.

Thinking he was done, I relaxed a little. Then he said, "Now, tell me about these spirits you say you claimed to behold."

I ignored the barb. "I understand a sighting is hard to grasp, Detective. I wouldn't have believed it myself if I hadn't seen them. At first, only one soldier appeared. Then Dee Dee spotted a lady ghost. That makes two."

With mouth agape he stared at me like I was crazy. "Okay. Go ahead. Tell me the rest." He wrote as I talked.

"Well, I don't have much else to say. One minute they were there, and the next they weren't. I do remember, though, I experienced a strange awareness when we went to the facilities right before we lay down. The ladies' room is close to the Andrews' Raiders display where Doc discovered the body. Oh yes, something else I thought seemed odd."

"And what would that be, Ms. Montgomery?" He twirled his cigar between his thumb and forefinger. Did he use the unlit cigar as a prop?

"The soldier was dressed in a Yankee uniform. Don't you find that outlandish, Detective? Why would a Yankee ghost want to hang around in the South?"

"You've got me." His caterpillar brows wiggled up and down, giving the illusion of crawling. "I appreciate your patience. I'm going to interview Ms. Lamont next, and I'd like for you to stick around until we're finished. Then I want to talk with both of you, as well as Mr. Pennington. Please try to stay out of the way while the officers work on the crime scene. I'll speak with you again in a little while."

With that, he stood up and left me alone to contemplate the past twenty-four hours. I felt like I'd stepped right into an episode of *The Twilight Zone.*

Dazed, I walked back to the quilt room to retrieve my cell phone and check for messages. I had one from Nana, my mother's aunt. She'd accompanied us to Marietta and was staying with a friend for a few days. I'd also received a call from Beau, my next-door neighbor. Beau and I have dated a little over these past six months. Last but not least, Harv, the editor of "Georgia by the Way," had left several messages. I bit the bullet, and called him first.

CHAPTER FIVE

H arv! Stop yelling. I couldn't call you back sooner. I've been kind of busy."

My editor is a wonderful guy at heart, and he'd do anything to help me out. He's just a big ole' teddy bear underneath that rough exterior of his, but he sticks to me like a cocklebur.

When it comes to his baby, as he calls "Georgia by the Way," he can get a little uptight and doesn't let up until my first draft of any assignment is on his desk for inspection. Having said as much, his boisterous ways played havoc on my last nerve sometimes.

"Have you accomplished your goals?" I heard him crunch an everpresent Tootsie Pop. The sweet treat became his vice after doctor's orders required him to give up smoking.

"Yes and no, Harv." Tirade expected, I held the phone away from my ear.

"What in the world do you mean?" That booming voice sounded like Harv stood next to me in the room.

"Calm down so I can tell you what happened." A 'hmph' shot through the phone.

"Yes, I've picked up a good story. No, I'm not sure when the article will be ready. We've experienced a bit of excitement, and the trip might take a little longer than we expected."

Over the next several minutes I explained what had transpired. I detected muttering as I hung up – something about being glad he didn't have to travel on assignment with me.

I flipped my cell phone closed. The world as I knew it yesterday, now felt surreal. I willed myself to call Nana. I wanted to make sure she was all right. Mama usually acted as my great-aunt's gate-keeper, but she wasn't here, so she trusted me to take care of her. Several times, this sweet little lady had wandered off on what she prefers to call "adventures." We've more aptly termed them "disasters."

Recently, Nana decided she wanted to enter the world of technology. So, she is the proud owner of a flip-phone designed especially for seniors. I caught her pressing several buttons before she hit the jackpot, so I set the menu to answer automatically when she flips the top open.

"Hello," a quivering voice answered.

"Nana, its Trixie. I noticed you called me earlier. Are you okay?"

"Oh, Trixie. Something terrible happened. I'm at the hospital."

"What's the matter? What hospital?" I could barely form the words. *Please Lord; remove this elephant from my chest. I can't breathe.* I wished I could blink my eyes and reach Nana as soon as possible.

"I'm all right, sweetie. Dora's taken a fall. After we went out to eat supper, we decided we'd go over to the bowling alley. They had a special - two games for the price of one. It was disco night, and they had all these brightly colored lights flashing and disco balls spinning. Those twirling things sure must have given her the dizzies!

"We were having a wonderful time, and everything was fine until Dora fell down and started flailing her arms and legs. The doctor said the flashing lights caused a seizure."

"How terrible." Immediate relief Nana wasn't lying in the hospital was followed by shameful guilt.

"Yes, it is! And that isn't the worst of it. Dora hit the floor like a ton of sand, and she broke her left hip." *That's a ton of bricks, Nana.* "You know that's been her bad hip for a long time." No, I didn't know about the bad hip, but the discrepancy seemed insignificant. "She's in surgery. They're not sure if she'll need a replacement. I'm waiting for the doctor. By the way, did I mention how cute he is? I think he's Italian."

"You didn't tell me about the cute doctor," I said, rolling my eyes.

The mistake was too late. Nana possessed an uncanny ability to detect when I'm eye rolling, and she never lets it slide.

"Don't roll your peepers at me, Missy."

No point in arguing with her. "Sorry. I wish I could come to the hospital, but something's happened at the museum. I won't be able to visit right away. Will you be okay until I arrive?"

My insides churned like an old-timey washing machine. I wanted to be with Nana as she waited for news about Dora. No matter how hard I tried, I couldn't envision Detective Columbo letting me go anywhere until he finished his interviews. I did the next best thing – I offered a prayer. *Please be with Nana and her friend and keep them safe. Dee Dee and I sure could use some comfort, too.*

"I'll be fine. The nurses and doctors have been so good to us. A nurse set me up in a little waiting room and gave me some snacks. Tommy, Dora's only son, lives in some foreign country. The name starts with a B, maybe Brazil or Britain. She told me he's a big wheel in a company over there. The doctor put a call in to him. You take care of your business at the museum and come on over when you can."

"Thanks, Nana. I'm so glad you're okay, and I'm sorry Dora fell."

"Thank you, Sweetie. I'm going to go and find out if I can finagle an update. When that nice young doctor comes out to talk to me, I'll put in a good word for you. A little competition wouldn't hurt Beau. I'll see you when you get here, dear."

"'Bye, Nana." I heard dead air and realized I didn't get the name of the hospital.

I flipped my phone closed and walked over to where Doc discovered the body. The activity resembled a bustling beehive. Officer Debra and Officer Rick were huddled, talking with each other. A redheaded woman dressed in jeans and a bright blue sweatshirt took pictures as fast as the shutter clicked.

As the EMT's carried the body out on the gurney, a lifeless arm flopped out from under the sheet, swung down, and dangled toward the floor. One of the techs reached down and nonchalantly tucked it back under. The hair on my own arms stood at attention.

CHAPTER SIX

Mr. Nice Suit, whom I assumed was the medical examiner, followed closely behind the techs. He turned around and addressed the police officers. "Tell Bowerman I'll call him later."

I was aware of my surroundings, but felt like I was in the midst of a horrible dream. Doc, standing next to a man I didn't recognize, surveyed the scene around him and appeared as displaced as I felt. We made eye contact, and I walked over.

"Trixie, this is Samuel Brooks. He's the chair of the museum board. Sammy's always been supportive of our cause, so I knew he needed to know what happened."

He flashed a toothpaste ad smile. "Sammy, this is Trixie Montgomery. She writes for "Georgia by the Way," and planned on writing a feature article on our ghosts. I hoped the publicity would be a shot in the arm for us; a good ghost story could renew interest in the museum."

Sammy and I shook hands. The man appeared to have stepped from a page of GQ magazine. He stood well over six feet tall. Up among the clouds, I imagined he experienced an air of supremacy over us mere mortals. A double-breasted suit with a pink dress shirt might be considered arrogant on some men. Not on Sammy. Olive skin, blue eyes, and salt and pepper hair completed the package. A thousand watt smile lit up his face.

I remember a time, after my divorce, I thought I'd never be interested in men again. Guess I was wrong.

"I'm sorry we have to meet under these circumstances, Ms. Montgomery. I must admit, the museum grapevine informed me of your visit. I suppose now that such a tragedy has occurred, you'll want to put your research off indefinitely?"

Ha! Sammy didn't have a clue when it came to Harv. If a story involved murder and mayhem, he anticipated the scoop more than ever. My editor isn't unfeeling, but he's a journalist, and that means he thinks like a reporter. *Get the story, no matter what!* is his rallying cry.

"I'm not sure what's going to happen, Mr. Brooks. The decision will be up to my editor." For a mere second his smile faded, but he quickly replaced it with blinding white teeth.

"Yes, of course."

He turned to Doc. "I'm going to talk with the officers to see if there's anything else I can find out. I need to inquire when we'll be able to open again for business. I'll call you later." He gave Doc a manly pat on the back. "Ms. Montgomery, it's been a pleasure to meet you. I'm sorry to make your acquaintance under these horrendous circumstances. I hope we'll have a chance to talk later." He left us standing alone. Two lost souls in a raging storm.

"Come on, let's go find somewhere to sit down." Gently guiding Doc by the elbow, I led him toward the sitting area in the foyer. Officer Debra hurried after us.

"Ms. Montgomery, I want to remind you Detective Bowerman needs to talk with you shortly." She hitched up her pants and settled her hand on her gun.

"I remember. We're just going to sit down for a while." I pointed toward the couch.

"Fine. But don't wander off too far," she warned.

I helped Doc get comfortable and sat down beside him. The silence between us was palpable. None of this made sense. Doc's face drooped, and his bottom lip quivered. I said a quick prayer. *Please Lord, don't let him cry.* Embarrassed to observe such an intimate moment, I looked up at the ceiling, down at the floor and anywhere else but his face. I wasn't sure what to do, so I gave his hand a consoling pat.

"Doc, I'm sorry you found the body. It must have been a shock." He looked over as if he'd just noticed me.

"Yes, yes. It was a terrible shock." He dropped his head into his hands.

"Do you know who the victim is?" I glanced around. Everyone was busy doing their jobs. No one paid attention to us.

"His name is Jacob Wallace. He's our handyman. Or rather, he *was* our handyman. We had to let him go. I was told he'd been making inappropriate advances toward some of the volunteers." Doc's face turned a bright shade of red. "What am I going to tell Penny? She'll be terribly upset. She's been functioning on her last nerve ever since these crazy incidences began."

I agreed. If Penny was the nervous type, this would really upset her. But, from my brief observation, I think someone, long ago, had stepped on her last nerve and ground that sucker to a pulp. Like Doc, I feared this might send her over the edge.

"What in the world was he doing in the museum?" I was thinking out loud and jumped when Doc said, "I don't know. Jacob was madder than a bull stung by a nest of hornets after I let him go. He said the accusations were all lies and I'd be sorry. He was right. I am sorry. Maybe if I'd investigated a little more before I fired him, the problem wouldn't have come to this."

"Don't blame yourself. I'm sure you made the best decision at the time."

"I didn't have a choice."

That surprised me.

"He'd been harassing Susan Gray, one of our board members who frequently volunteers. She happens to be the fiancé of Jeffrey Jones, who's also on the board. When Susan told Jeffrey what happened, Jacob's fate was sealed."

Before I could get more details, Officer Debra arrived and escorted us into Doc's office.

Shortly afterwards, Dee Dee followed Detective Bowerman into the room. "Good, we're all here." Columbo leaned against Doc's desk, studying his notes.

I sidled up to Dee Dee for comfort. Her frazzled appearance indicated she hadn't fared his inquisition any better than me or Doc.

Unlit cigar pointing at us each in turn, Bowerman's tone was somber. "We've ruled this death a homicide. I'm going to need you all to stay close by. Please leave any contact information with one of the officers so we'll be able to get in touch with you. I'm sure more questions will come up as the evidence is processed."

"Ms. Montgomery – Ms. Lamont, I realize you're from out of town, but I'd prefer you stay around for a few days. I'm sorry if this is an inconvenience to you." We nodded our heads yes in unison. He gave us one last once over as he chewed his unlit cigar. I almost confessed right then and there. He definitely had this Columbo thing down. "You're free to go now."

After he walked out of the room, I grabbed Dee Dee's arm. "Come on, Dee Dee! We have to go to the hospital."

"Ms. Montgomery! Not so fast," Officer Debra said. "I need to get some information from y'all first." We hurriedly gave her our cell phone numbers with the promise to call and tell her where we'd be staying. We also exchanged numbers with Doc and told him to let us know if he needed anything.

"What's Nana done now? Is she okay?" Dee Dee knew Nana way too well.

"Yes, thank God. It's her friend Dora. She fell at the bowling alley and broke her hip. She's in surgery right now."

CHAPTER SEVEN

A s soon as we settled in the car, I called Nana to find out the name of the hospital. Fortunately, the paramedics took Dora to Kennestone Hospital on Church Street, not far from the museum.

We found Nana camped out in the surgery waiting room. She stood in the corner talking with the most handsome specimen of human flesh I'd ever laid eyes on.

"Hi, Nana," I said. My heart pounded and my chest beat like a jackhammer.

"Hello, Sweetie." She gave me a big hug and pulled me right up next to the doctor. *What gorgeous eyes you have and what luscious lips.* I mentally slapped myself. *Girl, what are you thinking? You're here to check on Nana and Dora.*

"Dr. Rossi, this is my great-niece, Trixie. And she's single. Isn't she something?" As Dr. Hotty looked me over, I felt the heat travel from my neck to my ears. Nana moved to the top of my naughty list, knocking my ex-husband, Wade Montgomery III, down to second place.

"Hi. I told your aunt that Dora is out of surgery. We decided to go ahead and replace her hip. We'll keep her in ICU overnight, and if she does well she'll move to a room tomorrow."

"Has anyone been able to get in touch with her son?"

"I talked with him, and assured him she was doing fine and there was no need to fly back to the states at this time." His dreamy eyes scanned a whiteboard over my shoulder.

"She'll be in a regular room for four to five days. After her strength returns, we'll transfer her to the rehab floor where she'll stay another two weeks. If everything goes as planned we'll assess her progress and decide when she can go home. Ladies, do you have any more questions?"

Oh, yes! Questions like, *Are you married? How old are you? Where did you get those beautiful eyes?* Alas, my Southern upbringing wouldn't allow me to inquire out loud. Instead, I asked when we could visit Dora, and I was proud of myself for being able to focus while he told us we'd be able to visit her during the evening visiting hours. When he turned and walked down the hall, I noticed Dee Dee's gaze glued to his backside.

Nana smirked. "I told you. Admit he's one hot hunk." I swanny, I thought she licked her lips. I reached over and gave her a bear hug. "What's that for?" she asked as she straightened up her clothes.

"I'm so relieved you're not hurt. And yes, he is one hot hunk." Currently, that's how Nana described the men she found attractive. Lately, anyone who could grow a mustache seemed to pass her hunk radar.

"Wow, I think he's the most gorgeous man I've ever seen," Dee Dee said. She furiously rummaged in her purse and drew out what she called her "hot flash fan." The excitement and stress we'd experienced over the past twenty-four hours erupted. We broke into gales of laughter.

Nana shook her head, "Be quiet! Everyone's looking at us like we're crazy."

"You're right, but it sure feels good to laugh." I squeezed her to me.

We maneuvered our way through a maze of hospital hallways before we exited into sunshine as bright as a new copper penny. I rooted in my purse for my sunglasses.

"Hey, wait up y'all. I can't find my shades." Nana and Dee Dee turned around. They sauntered back to where I stood searching for the elusive specs.

"Want to borrow mine?" Dee Dee stuck her hand in her purse.

"That's all right. I know mine are in here somewhere." Truth is – I didn't think for one minute Dee Dee would find her glasses quicker than I could in the behemoth bag she called a purse.

"Here you go!" Dee Dee cheerfully handed me a pair of tortoise-shell sunglasses. A Cheshire Cat grin covered her face.

"Anybody hungry?" Nana asked. For such a petite little lady, my aunt ate like a bird – all the time.

"Yes!" Dee Dee and I shouted in unison. I realized neither of us had eaten anything substantial since Hemingway's the night before. I steered the car away from the square and the chaos of the museum.

"Let's go to the Big Chicken, I need comfort food." Dee Dee fiddled with the air conditioner trying to generate relief from the heat. It was a lost cause.

"Me, too. I'm hankering greasy chicken, mashed potatoes with gravy. Add two or three biscuits and that should do the trick. Are you game, Nana?"

"Sure, Sweetie. I may not be able to eat much – maybe a biscuit or two. I'm so worried about Dora. I can't wait to see her this evening. I'll feel much better when she's awake and talking to me." Nana wiped her forehead with one of her flowered handkerchiefs.

"I know it must have been scary when Dora broke her hip," I said sympathetically.

"Scary doesn't begin to describe my fear. Especially after she fell on the floor and started thrashing around. I had no clue what happened. I've never seen anybody have a seizure in real life, just on one of those doctor shows on the Discovery Channel."

In less than fifteen minutes we pulled into the crowded lot of the Big Chicken. Sunday afternoon in the South used to mean dinner after church at grandma's. Now, parishioners raced from services to the restaurants to see who crossed the finish line first. Rumor had it some churches began an hour earlier so their parishioners didn't leave before the benediction to beat the crowds.

The jam-packed parking lot bore testimony to these changes. Patience is not one of my better virtues, but I'd fervently prayed about this issue. This definitely constituted a practice situation. I swung into a space only to discover the area occupied by a little yellow Mini Cooper. It took another five minutes before we found a spot.

CHAPTER EIGHT

T he aroma of fried food wafted in the air. While we waited for a seat in the long line, I picked up a brochure on the origin of the Big Chicken. Dee Dee jabbed my ribs and interrupted the history lesson as we moved forward, and she signaled toward an empty table. I grabbed Nana and charged like General Patton on a mission. We barely beat out a family with two teenagers. Now, we'd have to tackle the lines at the order counter.

"Okay, here's the plan," Dee Dee said as she leaned in conspiratorially. "Nana, you and Trixie hold down the fort. Since I'm the largest, I have a better chance of bulldozing my way through the crowd. Tell me what you're hankering and I'll go get it."

Nana ordered first. "I'll just take a biscuit."

"Trix, how about you?" Before I opened my mouth to answer, Nana continued.

"And maybe a chicken breast – extra crispy – and mashed potatoes with some of that brown gravy."

"Sure thing, Nana." Dee Dee turned back to me.

Nana wasn't finished, yet. "Let's see. Get me some coleslaw to go with the potatoes. And a piece of lemon meringue pie for dessert."

"Are you through, Nana?" I asked.

"Well, yes honey. Oh, and don't forget a large sweet tea with lemon."

Dee Dee and I exchanged looks. I shrugged and silently answered her question. *I don't know where in the world she's going to put all of that food.*

"I'll order the same thing she's having – skip the pie." My stomach growled in agreement.

In a few minutes, Dee Dee forged her way back to the table loaded down with food.

Nana hesitated before eating. "Girls, haven't we forgot something?"

"Nana, what could we have possibly forgotten? We ordered enough to feed a small army." I looked around, wondering what we'd overlooked.

"How about giving thanks for all this food?" Nana folded her hands on the edge of the table.

"Oh my, you're right, would you please do the honors?" We bowed or heads in unison.

"Father, please be with all those who are in need. Bless this food to the nourishment of our bodies and our bodies to your service. In your son's name. Amen." Dee Dee and I added our amens.

For the next several minutes the only sounds heard from our table were mmmm's and ahhh's and the smacking of lips.

"Hey, Nana. How about sharing that piece of pie with us?" Dee Dee poised her fork ready to dig in.

Nana stared at her like she'd lost her ever-loving mind, but answered sweetly, "I don't think so."

"Well, all right, I'll go and get a piece for me and Trixie to share." She barreled her way through the crowd once more.

Nana reached over and took my hand. "Trixie, go ahead and spill the beans. I want to know what you've gotten yourself into over at the museum."

"What makes you think I've *gotten* myself into anything, Nana?" I said, but I already knew there was no need to argue with Nana. I wouldn't win anyway.

"Hmph, because I've known you since you were a baby. Remember?"

Right now, I'd take advantage of anyone who offered me a shoulder to cry on. Who better than someone who loves you? "You're right, I do have a lot on my mind. The director of the museum is Harv's good friend. This assignment is too important to mess up. I need this job, Nana."

"You've been through a lot, Trixie. Your mama and I are so proud of you. Just remember God is with you, even in the valleys." She grabbed my hand and gave it a squeeze.

Shortly, Dee Dee came back with not one - but two pieces of pure delight. So between bites of the best lemon meringue pie I've ever had the pleasure to eat, I filled Nana in.

I began to regret being so specific when I noticed her face turn paler than usual. Maybe her heart just wasn't as strong as it used to be. I lost all misgivings when she said, "My word girl, it's worse than I thought. Thank goodness I'm here to help you."

What *had* I gotten myself into? After Nana helped Dee Dee and me solve a murder, she'd come to fancy herself as an older version of Jessica Fletcher. She knows all the re-runs of *Murder She Wrote* by heart. I experienced an eerie sense of déjà-vu right before Nana spoke.

"Well, what's the plan?" Nana asked.

"The *plan* is to stay out of the way and let the cops do what they do best. Detective Columbo seems perfectly capable of handling the situation. Don't you agree, Dee Dee?"

"Huh? Oh yeah, sure, whatever you say, Trix." I glanced in the direction she was looking and discovered the reason for her distraction.

Detective Bowerman had entered, along with a couple of his cronies. He'd discarded the overcoat, but his rumpled suit wasn't much of an improvement. The unlit cigar protruded from his mouth. It was downright disgusting.

Ever the vigilant detective, he surveyed his surroundings with eagle eyes. I suppose he could have been searching for an empty table, but he appeared to be looking for someone to arrest. Then he spotted me. I quickly glanced away and hoped he hadn't recognized me. No such luck. Dee Dee waved to Detective Bowerman like he was our long-lost friend. I promptly kicked her in the shin, but it was too late; he made his way toward us.

Removing his cigar, he addressed us with a nod of his head. "Ms. Montgomery. Ms. Lamont."

"Hello, Detective," I replied. "This is my Nana—"

"Are you the detective who interviewed Trixie this morning?" Of course, Nana couldn't let it be.

"Yes, ma'am. And who are you?" He shot right back.

"I'm Belle, Trixie's aunt. Everyone calls me Nana." She smiled at Detective Bowerman and continued. "Detective, you sure are lucky my Trixie was at the museum this morning."

"Oh?" His facial expression didn't reflect someone who felt lucky. "Why would that be, ma'am?"

"Because. This is not the first murder Trixie's been involved in." Columbo's caterpillar eyebrows crawled up toward his forehead.

"Really?"

"That's right. She cracked a case wide open in Dahlonega last year. And I helped," she said proudly.

Oh-my-word! She sounded like the little girl on the old Shake and Bake commercial. You know, the one where she's helping her mother bake biscuits and at the end she states, "And I hel-lped" making helped a two-syllable word.

"Yes, Detective, and I was on the case, too," Dee Dee said with aplomb.

CHAPTER NINE

I don't think the conversation with Detective Bowerman went over as well as Dee Dee and Nana expected. Twirling an empty chair around, he sat down, eyes leveled at me. His arched brows led me to believe instead of seeing three astute amateur detectives; he ranked us right up there with the three stooges. He quickly confirmed my suspicion.

"Well, now. This is interesting, Ms. Montgomery. I don't recall any of this from our conversation this morning. Perhaps you were too modest to share this bit of information with me?"

His probing eyes bore right through me. I tried to swallow the lump in my throat, but it was like trying to swallow a cantaloupe.

Bowerman didn't wait for me to respond. "You can rest assured I'll follow up on this. Let me tell you right now, there will be no interference in my case. I don't want or need any amateurs messing around where they don't belong. Not only is it dangerous, but you could compromise the investigation. Do you understand, Ms. Montgomery?"

Well, shoot. Why ask me? I wasn't the one who brought up my involvement. He should interrogate Nana and Dee Dee. I'd deal with those two later. In the meantime, I didn't have a choice but to give him the answer he wanted. "Yes Detective, I understand."

"Good." He stood up, replacing the chair. "Don't forget to call the station and let them know where you'll be staying, in case I need to get in touch with you." Nodding again, he said a curt, "Good day, ladies." He stuck his cigar in his mouth, pivoted, and went on his way.

I turned to the two culprits. "Thank you. Between the both of you, I'm up to my neck in hot water."

"Well, who stuck a bee in *your* bonnet? We just sang your praises." Dee Dee came to their collective defense.

"Yeah, that's right Missy." Nana called me that when she wanted to remind me who was in charge. "Don't you go getting on your high horse with me. I just told the truth. No harm in that is there?"

I knew better than to answer a loaded question.

The crowd in the restaurant had thinned. I imagined the churchgoers headed home to take a Sunday afternoon nap, and I wished I was one of them. The night's activities were catching up to me. I didn't know about Dee Dee, but I could use a snooze. Between ghostly visits and Doc's harrowing dawn-thirty arrival, neither of us had slept much. At this point we didn't even have a place to lay our heads.

"Dee Dee, let's find a hotel for tonight."

Nana spoke up. "Take me over to Dora's first. I need to pack her some clothes to take to the hospital. And she has a couple of cats I'm sure she wants me to feed and water." Nana swigged the last of her iced tea. "Hey, why don't y'all sleep there for the rest of the afternoon until visiting hours? I know she wouldn't mind."

To tell the truth, I was too tired to go hotel hunting. I acquiesced quickly. "Nana, that sounds wonderful."

"Yes, it does. Lead the way young lady," Dee Dee said.

Of course, I thought she was talking to me. Before I could take my assignment, she grabbed Nana's elbow, and together they walked arm and arm to the car, leaving me to my own accord.

The drive wasn't far to Dora's, and soon we were pulling into her driveway. The gracious homes in the community shouted "old money." Whoever chose the dwelling's color must have loved blue bonnets. The rich blue presented a beautiful background for the magenta azaleas and rhododendrons framing the front of the house. A welcoming porch lined with rocking chairs invited the weary traveler to sit and rest a spell.

A rare breeze, filled with sweet summer perfume, ruffled our hair as we walked to the front door. The varied shades of green in Dora's yard reminded me of the Georgia hills on a spring day. God had painted a beautiful picture.

The inside of the house rivaled the outside. Dee Dee and I oooh'd and ahhh'd our way through the spacious cottage. The elegant house featured four bedrooms and two baths, dining room, living room, and kitchen. Exotic oriental rugs covered rich mahogany heart pine floors. Each room boasted crown moldings, wainscoting and wood ceilings. Wallpaper in a demure flowery pattern decorated the living and dining rooms. Unlike the understated common rooms, the bedrooms displayed deep, rich tones. I wanted to ask Nana the history later, but now I desired to lay my head down somewhere cozier than the hard, museum floor.

Since Nana already occupied one guest bedroom, Dee Dee and I picked between the two spare rooms left. We bade each other a "good nap," and I gratefully flung myself across the bed fully clothed. I fell asleep faster than a hound dog trailing a scent.

Next thing I knew, Nana gently shook me. I fumbled for the clock on the bedside table and glanced at the time. Instead of minutes, I'd been asleep for hours.

"Hey Sleeping Beauty," Nana cooed. "If we're going to see Dora this evening, we'd better get a move on. I packed her clothes, and Dee Dee toted them out to the car for me. We're just waiting on you."

Dee Dee stuck her head in the door. "That's right. And don't forget we need to stop somewhere and get some supper on the way to the hospital." Ever-practical Dee Dee.

"Y'all give me a few minutes, and I'll be ready." I yawned heartily and raised my arms above my head, loosening my achy spine. "I could stretch a mile if I didn't have to walk back."

Nana cackled. At least, it sounded like a cackle to me. "Hey, you stole one of my old sayings."

"Yes, I did. Now you two go find something to do while I make myself presentable."

"Geeze Louise. I don't think we have that much time, do we?" Dee

Dee grinned ear to ear. I threw a pillow at her, but my aim was off, and she escaped any serious damage. This time!

My phone dinged indicating a text message. It was from Harv and he wanted an update immediately.

CHAPTER TEN

We detoured into a drive-through and purchased burgers and fries. You'd have thought we'd eaten an adequate amount of grease for lunch, but we were in a hurry, and it was the only place quick enough. We finished our food in the hospital parking lot and headed toward ICU to check on Dora. Finding our way through the maze proved no easier than it had earlier that morning. We arrived a few minutes before visiting hours.

We plopped down to wait on a sofa that had seen better days and many bottoms. The cushion was so worn out I sunk lower than a worm in a wagon rut. Getting up would be next to impossible without help. I was glad Dee Dee sat beside me for more than one reason. She's been a rock in my life. Feeling maudlin, I reached over and patted her hand. She smiled and returned the gesture.

A bevy of visitors filled the waiting room. An older couple sat huddled together in the corner. Their features were drawn, and they held hands. I wondered who they worried about - their daughter, their son, or maybe a grandchild.

An extended family, from grandma to grandkids, sat across from us. The group were obviously celebrating a loved one's positive prognosis. According to the noise level, they were having a party – fixin's and all. I'd watched this scene played out before in hospital emergency rooms. This throng of family are often referred to in the south as "Mama and 'em".

A Good Samaritan told us visiting hours started, and everyone jumped up and headed to the double doors.

"Nana, do you want me to go in with you?" I put my arm around her shoulder and squeezed.

"That would be nice, dear. You can come too, Dee Dee."

"The sign says two visitors at a time, you and Trixie go ahead. I'll stay here and wait on you," Dee Dee instructed as she picked up a battered magazine.

Pleasantly surprised, we found Dora propped up, awake and talking. After we visited for a few minutes, I understood why Nana adored her. They were carbon copies. Reassured she was doing well, I excused myself to let them visit. To take our minds off more serious matters, Dee Dee and I spent the next several minutes expounding the virtues of "Mama and 'em".

Nana returned after the allotted time. Her eyes danced and she wore a huge grin, relieved her friend would be okay.

"She looks good doesn't she, Nana?" She nodded in agreement. "Come on. We'll take you back to Dora's and we'll go find a hotel."

Nana's eyes sparkled and her grin widened. "I mentioned to Dora y'all didn't have a place to stay, and she said, 'Nonsense! You let them stay at the house with you.'"

Tears sprang to my eyes. The thought of a quiet, relaxing place to stay thrilled my heart. Bowerman's warning on top of Harv's deadline mingled in my head, and I predicted we would need the extra rest for what awaited us.

Sunlight flooded my room. No! Wait a minute. This unfamiliar bedroom wasn't mine. As the cobwebs cleared from my mind, I remembered we'd spent the night at Dora's.

I emitted an audible groan, as I glanced at the clock and discovered it was only six in the morning. I pulled the covers over my head, not ready to face the day. Strange dreams had invaded my sleep, robbing me of a peaceful rest. During the nightmare the murder victim arose to haunt me, but when I saw his face it was that of my ex-husband, Wade. I wondered how an expert would explain that dream.

"Yooo-Hooo!"

I willed myself to sneak a peek from under the covers. Nana peered around the doorway. Her smile was way too bright this early in the morning. "Good! You're up."

"Do you know what time it is?" I pulled the covers back over my exposed head.

"Yep, it's after six. I overslept; I must've needed that extra shut-eye. I'm making home-made biscuits for breakfast." She sang off-key as she made her way down the hall.

I hauled my caboose out of bed, not bothering to change clothes. My jammies would do just fine for an audience with Nana and Dee Dee. Dragging into the kitchen, I noticed Dee Dee fared no better. Droopy eyed, bed-headed, pajama-clad Dee Dee sat at the table.

Dee Dee made a half-hearted effort to glance in my direction. "What are you grinning at? You don't look any better than I do." We took in each other's bedraggled appearance and burst into laughter.

Nana, dressed in a summer running suit, was cute as a button. Adorned in hot pink pants with a pink tee shirt, she looked like a spring flower. I knew a matching pink jacket existed. Nana never went any-where without a cover up, 'just in case.' Occasionally, she even wore a matching ball cap.

She hummed a catchy tune, as she stood at the stove and cooked a full-blown southern breakfast. The mingled smells came straight from heaven. My stomach growled in agreement. Nana heaped a plate with eggs, bacon, and homemade biscuits. She sashayed over and placed the feast before me.

"Here you go, 'shugah,' eat up! Y'all are going to need a heap of energy if you plan to investigate the murder at the museum."

"Nana! I told you I have no intention of getting involved. You heard Detective Bowerman warn me to butt out."

"Well, that's never stopped you before. Why should it now? And you have me and Dee Dee to help you."

Dee Dee sputtered coffee at Nana's declaration. "Uh, I don't know. Maybe Trixie's right. Detective Bowerman doesn't seem like somebody you'd want to cross. Actually, he looks kind of mean to me. Those thick hairy eyebrows give me the creeps." She wiped up the spewed coffee.

"I *know* I'm right. I don't want to hear any more nonsense about us investigating the murder." When she didn't answer, I repeated. "Did you hear me, Nana?"

CHAPTER ELEVEN

Nana turned around and looked me directly in the eyes. I was familiar with *the look*. I've known it since childhood, and it means I've definitely overstepped my boundary. She slowly, purposely laid down the spatula and placed her hands on her hips.

"Don't take that tone with me, Missy! Yes, I heard you. I might be old, but I'm not deaf. I won't mention the "M" word again. I thought it would be a boost for your article if you solved this murder like you did before." *So much for not mentioning the "M" word.* "Heaven forbid I try to help again." She turned around and continued cooking, her back straight. Even at her age, Nana kept herself in great shape.

"I'm sorry, Nana. I guess we're all on edge. Let's do something fun today. I don't have the heart to work on my story, and the museum is probably off limits anyway. Let's ride down to the square and hit some of the shops. Retail therapy always makes a girl feel better. What do you say?"

"Thanks for including me, but I think I'll sit with Dora."

"We could check on her first, the hospital's not out of the way." I took a big bite of biscuit loaded with strawberry preserves. The gooey goodness oozed out the side and fell onto my plate.

"No. I want to stay at the hospital. I feel responsible since she doesn't have any family close by." Nana removed empty dishes from the table.

"If that's what you want to do. How about you, Dee Dee? Are you up for shopping?"

"Does the Pope wear sneakers?" Dee Dee giggled at her own wit.

"I think the saying goes, 'Does the Pope pray?' Anyway, I'll take that for a yes. They have a lot of antique shops on the square. Maybe you can find something for Antiques Galore."

"I'd better call Sarah and tell her I'm not sure when I'll be back. I can't imagine what excuse I'm going to give her. What about my babies? Heaven only knows what they'll do without their mother. When I'm gone for more than a couple of days, they go off their feed." She wore the worried expression of a mother extremely concerned for her children. The fact of the matter was – her concern was for her cats – not her children.

"I'm sure Stephanie will be glad to take care of them. They'll be fine. Children are pretty resilient." I attempted to sound as serious as possible while I stifled a grin.

"I hope you're not being facetious, Trixie. You know how I feel about my babies. It's not a joking matter."

"Why don't we video chat with them, and you can see for yourself how they're doing." While Dee Dee considered that, I felt a tinge of guilt myself. "Speaking of babies, I need to call Mama and tell her we'll be staying a little longer than planned. She's taking care of Bouncer while I'm away. And Beau. I need to call him. Not only will he be worried, but I'm afraid he's going to be suspicious of how we wound up in another murder investigation. And if that isn't enough, I have to keep Harv updated." I heaved a big sigh.

"I'm sorry, Trix. But, better you than me," Dee Dee said.

After we finished breakfast, we returned to our separate bedrooms to get ready for the rest of the day. If we'd only known what was in store, we'd have pulled the covers over our heads and stayed in bed.

Within the hour, we were at the hospital receiving good news. Dora was awake and doing better than expected, with the possibility of being moved out of ICU later in the day. Nana insisted on staying, in case they moved her. We left her with instructions to call on her cell phone if she needed anything.

The minute we stepped outside, the sunshine proved we'd been blessed with another glorious day. The sun vied for a spot in a tropical island commercial. The azure blue sky was as clear as a crystal glass. A slight breeze tickled my skin. I relished the moment, aware the luscious breeze would be replaced with thick, sticky air later in the afternoon.

I conversed silently in prayer as I inserted the key into my temperamental Jeep's ignition and gave it a swift turn. Happily rewarded with the hum of the engine, I exhaled a sigh of relief. Shortly down the road, I decided to go-for-broke and give the air conditioner a chance, too. Semi-cool air shot out of the vents.

Dee Dee's elation was evident as she exclaimed, "Lo and behold, miracles never cease."

We basked in our good luck as we headed back to the Historic Marietta Town Square where a short twenty-four hours ago we experienced such a horrible day. I intentionally parked a comfortable distance from the museum.

"Come on, Dee Dee," I said as I grabbed my digital camera.

"I'm coming. Let me get my purse."

"Hey, can I put my wallet in your *purse* so I won't have to take mine?"

"Sure! There's plenty of room."

"You've got that right," I murmured.

"Admit it, Trix. It's come in handy more than once." She smirked, knowing she was right.

The historic square bustled with early morning tourists of every age, not to mention size and shape. A young couple strolled down the sidewalk as they held hands. Kids darted around the other tourists like they were on an obstacle course. Numerous shops surrounded the square. The historic district provided something for every taste and interest.

After you've shopped till you've dropped it's easy to find a variety of eateries to satisfy a healthy appetite. If you want candies, hand squeezed lemonade, or a variety of desserts – whatever you heart desires – you'll find it on the square.

My tummy voted for a break as we passed the ice cream shop. "Look! Hand spun ice cream. You get to choose the flavors, and then they'll mix them for you. Yumm, that sounds good. Want to go in and give it a try?"

We both decided on chocolate ice cream mixed with fresh

strawberries and Kahlua flavoring. The next fifteen minutes was an experience of pure bliss.

After we satisfied our sweet tooth, we meandered around the square. We discovered a quaint little shop; chock full of antiques and dust.

"Look, everything's half-price." Dee Dee opened the door releasing a wave of musty air.

I'd browsed for a few minutes when I heard Dee Dee – achoooooooooooo! Nobody can prolong a sneeze like Dee Dee. I headed toward the peculiar sound and literally bumped into her.

"Hey, Trix, look what I found!" Dee Dee held up a book so grimy I could hardly make out the title.

CHAPTER TWELVE

I took the book and read the title, "Capturing a Locomotive" by William Pittenger

"I think I'll buy it and see what I can discover about the event. That is, unless you want to buy it for your research."

"No. You go ahead. I can borrow it from you."

She searched the other spines, her nose so close I thought she was going to kiss them. "Oh, look." She grabbed another and pulled it out. "This one's titled "The Marietta History Museum." I'm going to get this one, too."

"I'd like to read it. The museum has a rich history."

Our purchases made, and our arms loaded down, we headed back outside into the sultry air.

Spotting a quaint little deli, we decided to stop for lunch. We chose a table where we could see the sidewalk outside while we ate a light salad. People-watching is a sport I've always enjoyed. As I surveyed a group of teenagers decked out with earrings, brow rings, and several other kinds of rings you could think of, my cell phone rang. Startled, I jumped off my chair like I'd received an electric shock. I answered quickly, thinking it might be Nana. "Hello!"

"Well, hello stranger! I thought you'd never call me. Oh, that's right, I called you." Harv guffawed, his passive aggressive comment rankling me.

"And how are you doing?" I met Dee Dee's questioning look, mouthing "Harv."

"Well, now that you asked, I'm not doing too good. We're on a deadline here and I'm waiting on a first draft from you."

I pictured him at his desk with his feet crossed on his desktop, sleeves rolled up, barking orders at poor Belinda, our receptionist.

"I'm trying. But I spent the night in a museum with a dead body. Then Nana's friend Dora fell and broke her hip. Dora's son is out of the country, so I feel responsible for both of them. Harv, truth be told, I'm frazzled."

"I'm sure you are, Kiddo"--Harv's pet name for me-- "I should be more sensitive, but I've got a magazine that's losing subscribers."

We spoke several minutes, or rather he talked and I listened. Before Harv said good-bye, he reminded me there was a story I needed to tackle. I wasn't in any hurry to follow up on this lead – especially after Detective Bowerman warned me to keep my nose out of his business. However, the best intentions can be forgotten.

My phone rang immediately after I hung up.

"Trixie? This is Doc. I need your help. I'm in trouble!"

"What's the matter?" My lunch churned in my stomach. Dee Dee's recently waxed eyebrows struck a questioning arch.

"Detective Bowerman brought me in for questioning. He referred to me as a "person of interest." Penny's in a panic, and I'm not doing so well myself. I'm really worried."

"Why? Have they found evidence linking you to the murder? They can't rely on your fingerprints; they must be all over the museum."

Dee Dee elbowed me and whispered, "What! What's going on?"

"Shhh." I mouthed, "I'll tell you in a minute."

"I'm afraid there's more to it, Trixie. Listen, would you and Dee Dee meet me somewhere? I don't want to talk about this over the phone."

Dee Dee, patience not being one of her virtues, was about to pull my arm off. If curiosity *could* kill, she'd be dead.

"Plan on it and I'll call you back if it's not copasetic." Dee Dee rolled her eyes at my use of the word copasetic. I rolled mine right back. "Where do you want to meet? We're on the square close to an antique shop named Magnolia Books and Antiques."

"There's a café on the far corner called Tara's. Can you meet me there in about twenty minutes?" Desperation laced his voice.

"Sure. We'll see you in a little while."

Trix, what did you get yourself into? Lord, help me. My hands shook and my palms were slick with perspiration. What did Doc expect me to do? And why was he in this predicament anyway? My taut shoulders violently quivered. The call must have shaken me more than I realized. An anxious voice interrupted my thoughts.

"Hey, girl. What are you so worked up about? Whatever's going on with Doc, you just might have to—"

"You're not going to believe this Dee Dee. Doc was taken in for questioning. He didn't want to explain over the phone, so he asked us to meet him in about twenty minutes."

"We promised bushy-eyed Bowerman we'd stay out of his way," Dee Dee said.

"My job could depend on solving this case. Meeting someone for coffee isn't the same as crossing police tape." Despite my brave exterior, genuine concern ushered us out the door.

A blast of steamy air hit us as we stepped outside and down the street. The sun beat mercilessly, heating the sidewalk. The temperature was on its way to hitting the nineties. Tourists looked as bedraggled as I felt. My throbbing knee forced me to move like a little old lady. It was slow going to the café. Dee Dee sensed my discomfort and slowed her pace to match mine.

Tara's appeared as an oasis in the desert. A blast of cool air welcomed us, and the inside of Tara's proved clean and inviting. Single roses in bud vases splashed color against white tablecloths scattered throughout the dining area. Bright blue, yellow and green accented the décor. A glass cabinet full of luscious desserts ran the length of the bar by the register.

Dee Dee and I agreed we were stressed, and everyone knows stressed spelled backwards equals desserts. We treated ourselves to a diet Coke and a slice of seven layer chocolate cake while we waited on

Doc. Between decadent bites of cake we discussed the murder at the Marietta History Museum.

While we waited, I observed our fellow patrons for entertainment. I've been told I'm nosey, but I don't see it that way. A writer must be observant. You never know when you might discover a story or acquire a new character.

For instance, consider the woman who just entered the door. I pegged her forty-something hoping to pass for twenty-something. Dressed in a short blue jean skirt, tube top, and white cowgirl boots, she made quite an impression. She sported blonde hair, complements of L'Oreal, and blue eye shadow applied to her entire eyelid. Think Robin Egg Blue.

I felt a jab to my shin. Dee Dee kicked me to get my attention. Doc came through the door. I waved to him and he headed over, looking awful. His hair was uncombed, and his clothes rumpled. He glanced our way and the corners of his mouth turned slightly upwards, making a feeble attempt at a smile. We scooted our chairs around to make room. He plopped down in the delicate seat and dropped his head in his hands.

CHAPTER THIRTEEN

D oc, do you want a drink?" I didn't wait for an answer. It was obvious he needed something stiffer than diet cola, so I sent Dee Dee to get him a high-test Coke.

He took a couple of sips, sat up and shared his story. "Like I said on the phone, I'm in trouble. Detective Bowerman took me to the station and questioned me for over two hours. I know I'm on top of his suspect list."

"What makes you think that, Doc?" I wasn't sure I wanted to know. "Maybe he just thinks you know more than anyone else, because of your position at the museum."

"He told me I was their person of interest." He emitted a nervous laugh and ran his fingers through his thinning hair.

Dee Dee interjected, her fork flinging bits of cake around the table. "Trixie and I discussed the fingerprint issue. They must be on everything in the museum. I can't imagine he'd base his suspicions on the appearance of your prints?"

I remembered he did have motive. "Did he discover you fired Jacob?"

Doc nodded, and with this confession, turned white as the flour Nana used for her biscuits. Like a bolt of lightning, it occurred to me Detective Bowerman must have something else on Doc.

I leaned forward. "Doc, what aren't you telling me?" My whispered question rustled the petals on the rose between us.

Doc's lips trembled. Silence prevailed before he shared an unbelievable tale. "It began a long time ago. After I finished my tour of duty in

Vietnam. I didn't want to come back to the states and face what so many fellow soldiers endured when they returned.

"So I naively decided to go as far away as possible. The Bahamas seemed like the perfect place to escape from reality." He sucked in a deep breath and continued.

"I wound up in Nassau. I worked a year on one of the local fisherman's boats. It wasn't the most glamorous job. I cleaned fish, scrubbed the boat, helped with the line fishing and any other job that needed done. It didn't pay much, but it was enough."

Doc took a long drink. I had no idea where this was going, but I could tell the memories were troubling this kind man. Dee Dee and I exchanged glances, anxious to hear the rest of the story. Doc gingerly sat the glass down on the table. He studied the container as if the answer to his problems lay at the bottom.

"There was a local man who worked on the same boat as I did. He stayed in trouble and made more enemies than friends. Mickel was extremely knowledgeable about the fishing trade and became an asset to the boat owner. I'm sure it's the only reason they kept him on. I tried to stay out of his way, and I did for a long time. Then one night we were in the same bar – The Golden Conch. He drank enough to kill a normal man, but it didn't kill him; it just made him meaner than the devil himself.

"Mickel badgered me because I wasn't an islander. He'd goaded me since I started working, and I guess he wasn't too happy I hadn't responded to his taunts. He went wild. He pushed me around, and when I didn't fight back, he sucker-punched me. I wasn't going to stand by and let him beat me to a pulp so I fought back." Beads of sweat dotted Doc's forehead.

"When he saw I wasn't going to give up, he pulled out a machete, and charged like a raging bull. Without thinking, I grabbed the closest thing I could reach, and hit him over the head. I wanted to stop him. I didn't mean to kill him – it was just a beer bottle."

Doc dropped his head. I saw tears in his eyes before his hands covered his face. Maybe it was emotional exhaustion, or maybe he didn't want us to see him cry.

Dee Dee shrugged her shoulders, and I knew what she thought. How could this gentle man have killed someone – even in self-defense? A thousand questions flowed through my mind.

While we gave him a few minutes to collect his composure, we ordered another drink. I ordered Doc a piece of raspberry cheesecake. I hoped the treat would comfort him in some small way.

Dee Dee and I made small talk and sat quietly out of respect for Doc, but I couldn't help wondering. I'd gauged Doc for a gentleman. Was I wrong? He'd just admitted he was guilty of murdering before. Was it possible he'd felt threatened enough again?

CHAPTER FOURTEEN

A re you telling us Detective Bowerman found out about your barroom...um, brawl?"

"Yes, he did. Interpol, I guess. It happened so long ago; I haven't thought of Mickel in years. At the time, I feared I might spend the rest of my days locked away in a Nassau prison.

"But, it seems this man was hated by a lot of people – some in high places. After spending less than six months behind bars, without a trial, they released me. They demanded only one condition for my release – leave the island. I happily complied. I never wanted to see that place again.

"This was a wake-up call for me. I decided then and there living in the United States was a wonderful privilege. I turned my life over to God, and determined to put the terrible experience behind me. I'd pretty much convinced myself it never happened – until the detective confronted me."

"Doc, I'm sorry you're going through this. What can we do to help?"

"I heard you solved a murder in Dahlonega, and I hoped you'd help me. I don't know where else to turn."

I thought of the harsh words I spoke to Nana this morning. I promised I wouldn't get involved in this murder, and Detective Bowerman's warning resonated. I knew very little about Doc, and now he had confessed to killing in self defense. But, I wasn't convinced the man who sat across from me could be a cold-blooded killer.

I looked over at Dee Dee. She shrugged her shoulders, which didn't give me much to go on. If I helped Doc, I'd have to eat the words I'd spoken to Nana this morning. *Lord, what should I do?*

I didn't hear a distinct voice, but a feeling of peace settled over me. I knew the answer. I had to help Doc. I'd want someone to do the same for me.

"I'll do what I can. I don't even know where to start," I said.

Dee Dee took this as a cue to share her thoughts. "What about other people who might have a motive to kill Jacob? Trixie, we could make a list of acquaintances who Doc thinks might have it in for him." She rummaged around in her purse.

"A list is a great idea. Doc, do you know of any enemies Jacob made while he worked at the museum?" I sipped my now watered-down soda.

"Yes. Yes, I do." Doc's face brightened. He pushed the cheesecake away that he'd only picked at.

Dee Dee found a pad, and with pen poised said, "Go ahead Doc. I'm ready."

"Well, let me think. There's Susan Gray. She's a board member and the main reason I fired Jacob. He made unwanted passes at Susan and harassed her, to boot." Doc's face turned beet red. "She's engaged to marry Jeffrey Jones. Not only is he a board member, too, he's a big supporter of the museum as well as a historian and collector of Civil War memorabilia. I guess Jacob didn't think she'd tell anyone, but she pretty much shouted it from the rooftops. Jeffrey was hopping mad and demanded I get rid of Jacob. I would have done it anyway, but he insisted I fire him." Taking a long swig of his high-test Coke, he wiped his brow with a dainty paper napkin.

"Write down all those names." I watched Dee Dee scrawl. "Not only did Susan have a reason to dislike Jacob, but her boyfriend, Jeffrey, did too. Maybe he wanted to dispose of him for good." I began to perspire; Southern ladies don't sweat. The air conditioner had either quit, or couldn't keep up with the heat and humidity building outside as the afternoon approached.

Dee Dee wrote furiously. "Got 'em down. Anybody else you can think of Doc?" She held up her glass and showed the waitress we all needed a round of drinks.

He rubbed his forehead. "I don't know. I feel like my head is full of cotton and I can't think."

"Who are all the board members? Maybe one of them had an axe to grind," I prompted.

"We only have five at this time. Samuel Brooks, you met him yesterday. He's the acting director. Gloria Hamilton, she's the one Penny told you about. You remember – her purse went missing. She's determined to wreck havoc in my life. She wants her son, Steven, to take over my position when I retire and she's hoping it will be soon." Doc let out a big sigh.

"Go on, we're listening." Dee Dee encouraged.

"I've already mentioned Susan Gray. She's the one Jacob harassed. And of course, me. I'm on the board."

"There is another person I haven't mentioned, but I don't think she would hurt a flea, much less commit murder. When I found out Jacob made unwanted advances toward Susan I wondered about someone else. I asked Marianne, our receptionist and bookkeeper, if he'd bothered her. She denied it at first, then later admitted he'd harassed her, too." Sweat continued to bead on Doc's brow.

"All right, that's a start. Can you get me their addresses?"

Dee Dee gave me a funny look. I know she was thinking "what do we need their addresses for" and I wondered the same thing. Was I willing to put myself in danger by investigating this murder?

CHAPTER FIFTEEN

I decided the challenge was worth the risk. I encouraged Doc to continue.

"That's easy, they all work downtown. You can easily catch them at their businesses if you want to talk to them. Except for Gloria, who lives on the edge of town within walking distance." Doc drained his refill of Coke. I'd lost count of how many he'd guzzled.

"Dee Dee, did you get all this? We'll need it later for reference. Neither one of us have the memory we used to."

She gave me a scathing stare. "Speak for yourself – I take Ginkgo biloba faithfully. That is, when I remember to. You should, too, memory herbs might do you some good."

I shook my head. Leave it to Dee Dee to add some humor to the difficult task we faced. I don't know what I'd do without her.

I noticed bags under Doc's bloodshot eyes. "Doc, why don't you walk back to the museum, and Dee Dee and I'll figure out where to start. I need to check on Nana. We'll stop by the museum later on today."

Doc raised his head slowly and offered me a half-smile. "Thank you so much, Trixie. And you, too, Dee Dee. I don't know what I'll do if the killer isn't found." He wiped the moisture from his brow with the now shredded napkin that came with our refreshments. "I'm anxious to tell Penny you've agreed to help. Your involvement will give her some hope to hang on to. My heart aches to see her so upset."

I gave Doc a little pat on his arm. "What a great idea. Why don't you ask her if she can think of anyone who might want to kill Jacob Wallace?"

"Dee Dee, write down our numbers for Penny in case she thinks of anything?"

"I'd be happy to, boss." She grabbed her pen and pad and handed our contact information to Doc. She took her job as my scribe seriously.

We bade Doc good-bye and walked back to our car. Though the air remained muggy a slight breeze tickled my arms.

Downtown historic Marietta represented a fading part of Americana. In the center of the square, townsfolk moved past park benches. I took a stroll down memory lane, as the children chased each other around a statue of a soldier on horseback, standing guard over them.

"Why the melancholy smile, Trix?"

We stepped back as the kids circled us then continued on. "Thinking how much I miss those carefree days." I changed the subject to more serious matters. "I'm concerned about Doc. I'm not sure where to start. We can ask questions, but will our investigation be enough?

"That's a good question," Dee Dee said. "But our help gives him hope. Everyone needs hope in their lives." We stopped at the curb to wait for the light to change. "It hasn't been long since you helped me out of a hopeless situation. If you hadn't been there, I might be sitting in prison for a murder I didn't commit."

No one is immune to hopelessness. After Wade divorced me, I had sunk to the depths of despair. Dee Dee stood steadfast with me through the tough times.

"I remember my circumstances when we went on the trip to the Gold Rush Days. With the Dahlonega assignment being the last before my six-month probation, I felt hopeless, too. I suppose we all face the possibility of defeat head-on at some time during our lives."

Dee Dee grabbed my arm and pulled me toward the curb. "Chin up, girlfriend. We'll help out Doc and then get you back on the beat."

In a few minutes we were in my Jeep and on the way to the hospital. I jiggled all the buttons, but couldn't get the air conditioner to work. I hoped the double duty deodorant I'd applied this morning worked.

"What are you doing, Trixie? We passed that store a minute ago." Dee Dee's voice raised an octave "We're going in circles."

"These are one way streets, and I'm looking for the road we took yesterday." I quickly pulled over into the next lane and hung a sharp right.

"Are you trying to kill me?"

"Sorry. I just remembered the turn."

Dee Dee pulled her seat belt a little tighter and grabbed the handle above her door.

"Aw, come on. I'm a good driver."

She made some weird choking sounds.

"What about the collection of tickets you've accumulated since moving back to Vans Valley?

"The only reason I've received so many is because Vans Valley's a small town, and their patrolman has the hots for me." I winked, and she grinned.

"I'm telling Beau on you." Dee Dee reached over and patted my arm. "I'm glad you're having some fun. I know you felt pretty low after Wade left."

We chatted about my new life for a few minutes, until at last, we pulled into Kennestone Hospital's parking lot. I snatched my cane for support. Dee Dee grabbed her gigantic bag. The multi-storied brick hospital towered above our heads as we walked to the entrance. This time around, we maneuvered through the maze of hallways much easier.

Dora sat up in bed, dressed in a pretty pink gown. I was pleasantly surprised. "Well, look at you, Dora." She rewarded me with a big smile.

"Hi, Dora. Hi, Nana," Dee Dee chimed in. "Where is Doctor Hotty?" Nana and Dora laughed. I didn't think it was *that* funny.

"Oh, don't worry. He'll make his rounds soon." She poured a drink of water for Dora and handed the plastic cup to her. "Why don't you stay a while, Trixie? I know you'd love to see him again." It might be true, but she garnered way too much pleasure in trying to fix me up. I rolled my eyes. Besides, she knew I'd been dating Beau.

"I saw that, Missy. Don't you roll those eyes. I'll catch you every time." True to her word, she always did. Almost always.

I surveyed the bland walls and the scarred linoleum floor. Why couldn't hospitals jazz up the décor with cheerful colors? At least the nurse's uniforms had evolved into colorful garbs, instead of the drab white they used to wear.

The door opened wide and in walked a small, diminutive looking nurse. She reminded me of a bunny rabbit until she opened her mouth. "Out! Everybody out!" She barked the orders. "I have to check Miss Dora's sutures and change her bandages and she doesn't need an audience."

CHAPTER SIXTEEN

No one budged, but she wasn't giving up. "Shoo. Scoot. I won't tell you again to leave." Nurse Patton rounded us up like a herd of cattle and guided us toward the door.

Dora called out, "Don't go home. Please come back in when she's finished, we haven't even had time to visit."

We assured her with a chorus of affirmations we wouldn't go. We stood outside and waited.

"Wow, what an attitude." Dee Dee stuck out her tongue at the door and blew.

"That's not very grown up, Dee Dee. But I can't say she didn't deserve that raspberry. She acted like she ate lemons for breakfast."

In a few minutes the nurse stepped outside and addressed us curtly, "You may go in now. But do not tire out my patient. She needs her rest." With a lift of her chin, she dismissed us lowly minions.

Nana nudged me. "Look!" She pointed toward the nurse walking away from us. A trail of toilet paper followed her down the hallway, stuck to her shoe. We doubled over in laughter. "Serves her right," Nana said.

We hustled back into Dora's room to relay the incident. "She's not so bad. She just doesn't have any people skills," Dora said.

"Nana, Dee Dee and I are going over to Gloria Hamiltion's to interview her for the article I'm working on. Do you want to come with us?"

"No thanks. I'll stay with Dora. Why don't you pick me up on your way back?"

Dora sat up a little bit straighter. "Are you talking about *the* Gloria Hamilton?"

"She's on the museum board and has a son named Steven. Do you know where she lives?" I made eye contact with Dee Dee. I hoped she got the message not to mention the real reason for our visit with Gloria. I wasn't ready to tell Nana.

"According to Doc Pennington, the museum director, she holds a lot of weight in this town," Dee Dee said.

"Hmph, she thinks she does anyway. She walks around with her nose stuck up in the air, like she's better than the rest of us. Well, I'm here to tell you she isn't." Dora struggled to rearrange her pillows. Dee Dee beat me to assist her, fluffing and readjusting them.

"Gloria married into money. We went to school together, and her family was dirt poor. I'm not saying there's anything wrong with being poor, but she wants everyone to believe her family was one of the blue bloods. But in reality, it was her husband's relative who was one of the founders of Marietta."

Dee Dee and I looked at each other. "Can you tell us where she lives?"

"Don't know the address, but if you'll get me some paper, I'll draw you a map."

Our hand drawn map in hand, Dee Dee and I passed the nurses' station where Nurse Patton stood. Her stare bore into us, like we'd planted the toilet paper on her shoe. We giggled like schoolgirls.

Painted white with forest green shutters, regal was the best way to describe the historic house we approached. It was easy to picture someone like Gloria Hamilton living there. Tall columns stood like sentinels along the front porch. The second and third floors boasted French doors that opened up to expansive balconies.

Swings hung at each end, and wicker rockers dotted the rest of the front porch. A variety of colorful bushes filled the front yard. As I strolled down the rock walkway, the sweet smell of fragrant gardenias lingered in the air.

"Wow. She may have grown up poor, but she's come a long way. This beautiful home reeks of old money. Wouldn't you say so, Trixie?"

"It definitely says money from the outside. I'm anxious to see the inside." We didn't have long to wait. I reached out to ring the bell, but the door flew open before I had a chance. A woman, who I assumed was Gloria, stood in the doorway. She was tall, stout and dressed to the hilt. Gloria Hamilton resembled every bit the lady of the house.

"If you're selling anything I don't want any."

"No, we're not selling anything Ms. Hamilton. I'm Trixie Montgomery." I handed her a business card. "I write for "Georgia by the Way" and I'm working on an article about the Marietta History Museum. I'd love to interview you. I understand you're an authority on all things Marietta. If your time allows, that is." I was proud of myself for remembering how to make an interviewee feel at ease. Gloria seemed to relax, but she glanced at Dee Dee skeptically.

I thought fast. "This is my assistant Dee Dee Lamont."

Stepping back, Gloria let us inside. "I think I can afford you a few minutes. I'm on my way to a committee meeting in a short while." She glanced at her watch. "We'll need to hurry." She led us through the marble foyer and into a sitting room stuffed with antiques.

"Gloria. May I use your first name?" She nodded affirmation and I offered a compliment, more genuine than the last. "Your furniture is beautiful."

Dee Dee nodded. "I own an antiques store and recognize excellent craftsmanship."

Gloria sat up a little straighter. "I understand your admiration. They're family heirlooms. I'm so proud of them." She didn't say whose family – just family. "I'm sorry I can't offer you refreshments, but this is Amy's day off. What do you want to know about the museum?"

I asked a few questions about the town in general, and Gloria happily supplied information. And then I changed directions.

"Gloria, is it true your purse disappeared while you were at the museum?"

Her eyebrows arched until they resembled tiny umbrellas. "Who told you that?" I expected her to show us to the door, but she surprised me when she continued. "Yes, it was *stolen* and there was no one around but Penny Pennington. I won't go as far as to say she took it, but who else could have taken it? The ghosts?"

CHAPTER SEVENTEEN

S peaking of ghosts." I shot Dee Dee a sideways glance, and she returned an encouraging nod. "Have you ever seen any ghosts at the museum?"

Gloria lowered herself to perch on the edge of a beautiful sage green brocade loveseat. "No. Of course I've never seen any ghosts." The way she answered you'd have thought I'd questioned her sanity. "Doc made up all that ghost talk to try and boost traffic at the museum. I don't believe one bit of it."

I didn't believe in ghosts either until the other night. Now, I'm not so sure. "Gloria, is it true your son is the next logical choice to take over as director?" I took a big chance with this line of questioning. Dee Dee confirmed this when she looked at me like I'd lost my ever-loving mind.

Gloria's face scrunched up like a prune and turned a strange shade of pink, I assumed her color change confirmed what Doc suspected. "Well, someone like my son needs to take over and clean house, the books haven't balanced for years, and no one can figure out why."

She stood up and walked toward the door. "Your time is up. I need to leave for my gathering. It was nice meeting you ladies." She ushered us out the door faster than a lizard catching a fly.

"I think you touched a nerve, Sherlock." Dee Dee chuckled, as we hurried down the sidewalk. "Let's find something to eat and figure out our next step."

"We could return to the Big Chicken and consume some comfort food for the soul." We drudged back to the car in the sweltering heat.

Thankfully it started on the first try, and after a few minutes cool air blew from the vents. *Thank you Lord for small miracles.*

The Big Chicken wasn't packed, but boasted plenty of customers. We ordered our food and found a table in the back corner. I'd taken my first bite and licked my fingers when my phone rang. I wiped off the grease then checked to see who called.

"Hey Harv."

"How are things going? Is your story on the murder coming along?"

"I'm doing as much as I can, Harv. I have to follow it from afar. The lead detective warned me to keep my nose out of his business." He didn't need to know we'd decided to ask a few questions ourselves.

We talked a few more minutes before, Belinda, Harv's receptionist interrupted with a bigger problem. "Okay, Kiddo. Check in with me tomorrow and be careful."

"What do you think we should do next, Dee Dee?"

"If you want the truth, I suggest go home to Vans Valley." I didn't blame her for wanting to tuck tail and run – I did, too, but the stack of unpaid bills kept me going.

Instead, we decided to pick up Nana at the hospital and head for our temporary abode Dora had so graciously offered. We ordered a take out plate for Nana before we left the Big Chicken.

When we returned to Dora's room, we found her asleep and Nana dozing in the chair. I hated to wake her up, but she needed to go home and get a good night's rest in a real bed. I was confident she'd want to come back tomorrow. We left Dora a note and tiptoed out. Nana stopped at the nurse's station to tell them she was leaving.

"What's that wonderful smell?" Nana asked after we settled in the car. "I swanny, I believe it's fried chicken." She looked around the car.

"You're right, Nana. You have the nose of a bloodhound," Dee Dee said. "We ate at the Big Chicken for supper and figured you'd enjoy a little night time snack." Dee Dee held up the take out box. Nana grabbed it.

Dusk settled in by the time we left the hospital parking lot. With the windows rolled down, the heat proved bearable. On our drive back to Dora's, the night insects sang their songs. Fragrant air blew in, laden with the sweet smell of honeysuckle and privet hedge. The car filled with talk and laughter. The chaos over the last couple of days had put a damper on our spirits, and the levity was a welcome relief. It was short lived.

We opened Dora's front door to a scene of destruction. Couch cushions littered the floor, and overturned potted plants spilled their soil across the room. Desk drawers lay open, their contents carelessly scattered about.

"Oh, no," Nana exclaimed. "What in the world happened?"

"I don't know Nana, but we don't need to be in here." I grabbed Nana by the arm and backed her out of the house. Dee Dee dialed 911. In less than ten minutes a squad car pulled up. Out jumped Officers Roach and Trapp, the duo in blue.

After the officers made a thorough sweep of the disheveled house, they allowed us to go back in. Nana walked a little weak kneed. I supported her with my arm. Dee Dee's face had lost a good portion of its color. The pit of my stomach agitated like an old butter churn. Why had someone decimated poor Dora's house?

"Ms. Montgomery, could you please tell us what happened?" Officer Roach opened her tablet and grabbed a pen from her pocket. Officer Trapp continued to go through the house. I told her what little I knew. My head shot up when the front door flew open.

"Well, Ms. Montgomery. What have you gotten yourself into now?" Detective Bowerman stood in the doorway. His hair stuck out in all directions. As usual, his clothes looked as if he'd slept in them. He twirled his ever-present unlit cigar between his fingers. What was he doing here?

CHAPTER EIGHTEEN

U h, what are you doing here, Detective?"

"I'll ask the questions Ms. Montgomery." He worried his hair with his fingers. No wonder it stuck straight up.

Nana, Dee Dee and I sat side-by-side on the couch. "Can you ladies tell me what happened tonight?" We answered in unison, and he shot out a stogied hand. "One at a time, please."

We didn't have much to tell him, except that we'd come home to the obvious mess, so Detective Bowerman walked through the house while the techs lifted fingerprints from various objects in the room. Time passed as slow as molasses on a cold winter's night as we waited on the detective.

"I think we have what we need. You can access the other rooms now." Bowerman told us, and then one of the officers came over and whispered something in his ear. He continued, "We've performed a detailed search and found no sign of anyone. I still have some concerns. When this much destruction is evident, it usually means someone was looking for something. At this point, we're not sure what and if they've found it. Also, none of the other rooms have been disturbed which makes me think you might have surprised the burglar."

My heart made an unplanned trip into my throat. If what he stated was true, it's possible whoever broke in would come back to finish the job.

"That means they might return." Dee Dee's voice quivered.

"Yes ma'am. That's a concern. We checked all the windows to

confirm they're locked. When we leave, please lock up and check the dead bolt. I'm not trying to scare you. I just want you to be safe. Truth is, they're unlikely to come back, but I'll have the officers patrol the area throughout the night."

The officers packed up their equipment and left us to deal with the aftermath of the break in.

"I don't know about you girls, but I sure don't feel like sleeping." My nerves felt like electricity coursed through them, and thoughts swirled through my mind like leaves in a whirlwind.

"Me neither," Dee Dee said. "What do you think, Nana?"

"I couldn't sleep if I had to. Let's stay up for awhile. I'm so worried about the break in." She wandered around, picking up undamaged items and returning them to shelves. "Dora was nice enough to let us stay and now someone has broken in and destroyed her belongings. I sure hope she doesn't think it had anything to do with us."

We spent a while cleaning, and collapsed over a pot of hot tea, discussing the events of the last couple of days. Within the hour Nana's head fell over to the side and she snored loud enough to wake the next town over.

"Come on Dee Dee. Let's help Nana to bed. I think I might be able to sleep now." I doubted I could, but I wanted to lie down and rest. My body ached from weariness.

"That sounds like a great idea," Dee Dee said. She went over and shook Nana's shoulder. "Nana. Off to bed we go."

Morning promised to bring a better day when the dawn broke into a luminous show of daylight. Nana cooked another good ole' down home southern breakfast loaded with fat and cholesterol. Dee Dee grabbed the syrup and poured a liberal amount over her second stack of pancakes.

"Please pass the syrup, Dee Dee." I drowned my pancakes in a river of the sweet sugary liquid. I took a huge bite and savored the flavor as it passed over my taste buds. No wonder they called it 'comfort food.'

"Nana, are you going to sit with Dora today?" I swirled around another bite and popped it into my mouth.

"Yes, I'd like to stay with her again. Did y'all go to Gloria's just to interview her for your story? I have a feeling you had an ulterior motive."

"I don't want you to worry, but Doc wants me and Dee Dee to help him. Detective Bowerman informed him he's a person of interest in the case, and after all this happened last night—"

"I knew it. I knew it. I knew it." Before I finished explaining, Nana did a crazy little dance around the kitchen. "I knew you wouldn't be able to keep out of the investigation. What do you want me to do?"

I didn't want her to do anything. She could help by not helping, but I couldn't bring myself to say that to her. "Uh, staying with Dora and making sure her needs are taken care of will be a great help."

"How in the world am I going to tell Dora someone broke into her house? She doesn't need any added stress." Nana's brows knitted with worry.

"Let me and Trixie explain everything to her when we drop you off," Dee Dee suggested. She pushed her plate back and wiped her mouth. Nana filled our coffee cups with fresh brewed coffee.

"By the way, Trixie, remember that book I found about the history of the Marietta Museum?"

"Sure, you found it next to the book on Andrews' Raiders."

"That would be the one," Dee Dee replied. "When I couldn't sleep last night, I read some from the book and it's interesting. Did you know the museum was a hotel at one time? The owners originally named it the Fletcher House and later changed it to the Kennesaw Hotel. It was owned by a northern couple who had three daughters."

"Harv told me it had been a hotel at one time."

"The lady at the bookstore said the owner, Louisa Fletcher, kept a diary. The Fletchers lived in the hotel during the Civil War."

"That is interesting. I'd give my right arm to get my hands on that." I absently rubbed my arm. "Not really, but you know what I mean. I wonder if Doc could acquire a copy."

"Let's ride over to the museum and ask him if he knows anything about it."

We decided to tell Dora about the break in later, there was no reason to worry her until we knew more from the investigation. After we dropped Nana off at the hospital, Dee Dee and I drove to the museum.

It was hard to believe only a few days had passed since our arrival. Less than seventy-two hours since we'd arrived, we had found ourselves knee-deep in a murder investigation.

I surveyed the three-story, red brick structure that held years of history. Not only did it house memorabilia from years gone by, it contained history from the people who lived there since its conception. If only the walls could talk.

The old Marietta train depot stood to the left of the museum and housed the visitor's center. To the right stood another historic building, home to the Gone with the Wind Museum. An abandoned railroad track ran parallel to the buildings. I imagined Civil War era ladies in their dresses with hoop skirts, and men driving carriages and wagons down the streets.

"Trixie, did you hear what I said?"

"Sorry. I was daydreaming about times gone by."

"I said, wouldn't it be fun to visit the Gone with the Wind Museum?"

"Maybe we can." We entered the building, and took the elevator up to the second floor. As the doors opened, I was once again transported back to a time when life was much simpler.

A young woman, I guessed to be in her thirties, sat behind the mahogany counter. She stood when we approached. "My name is Marianne, may I help you?" With long blond hair and a petite build, she was a pretty little thing.

"Is Doc here?" I looked around to see if I could spot him.

"No. You just missed him." She checked a sign-in board on the wall behind her. "He should be back within the hour. I'd be glad to give you a tour."

"I'm Trixie, this is Dee Dee. We'd love to look around." This was a good time to talk with her and see if she knew anything that might help Doc. Dee Dee gave me the *eye*. I don't think she was as anxious to go on another expedition of the museum.

"Why don't I browse in the store, Trix, while you go with Marianne?"

"Suit yourself." I didn't blame her. I'd seen more than enough of the museum myself.

CHAPTER NINETEEN

We began in the Andrews' Raiders room. A silhouette of a man stood at the window and looked out over the railroad tracks. The scene seemed eerily realistic. Marianne explained Andrews' Raiders were a band of northern spies who came to Marietta with one goal. They stole a southern locomotive engine, the General, with the intention of destroying the tracks along a much used supply route. Their plans foiled, Andrews and his gang ran for the hills. His pursuers ultimately caught and hung him.

"What did you say your name is?"

"Trixie Montgomery. I write for "Georgia by the Way" a historical magazine. We like to say, *where the past meets the present.*"

Marianne's eyes widened. "You're the one who stayed overnight at the museum while the murder took place." She sat down in a chair that was part of a display. I knew enough about museums to understand it wasn't kosher to touch any of the items. "That must have been horrible. But I can't say I'm sad Jacob is gone."

I grabbed a chance to jump in and ask some questions. "Marianne, have you heard the police fingered Doc as a person of interest?" Her eyebrows arched and her eyes widened.

"No. I didn't."

"He's in big trouble. Do you have any information that could help us find the real killer?" I recognized I was in deep over my head – questioning her about a murder. *Please Lord, help me help Doc.*

At first, I believed she was going to clam up. Then a lone tear slid down her cheek. "I'll support Doc any way I can. He's been so good to me." She swiped the tear from her face. "Jacob was a jerk. He'd worked at the museum for less than six months when he started to make moves on me. Moves I didn't want."

"Did you tell Doc?" I remembered Doc said Jacob had made advances toward Susan. The guy must have hit on everyone.

"No. Jacob threatened me," she said. "I should have told Doc, but Jacob had something on me. He said he'd expose my secret to Doc and the board. It scared me. I have a daughter I care for by myself, and I was afraid I'd lose my job if Jacob let this out."

What information did Jacob have on her? "Marianne, what did he discover that made you keep quiet about something as horrible as unwanted passes?"

She started to cry in earnest, "I can't tell you," she sobbed. I managed to find a clean tissue for her. She sniffed and wiped her nose. "But the time has come to tell Doc."

I had to find a way to observe the conversation if I planned to help Doc. "Do you want me and Dee Dee to sit in with you? The more information we have on Jacob could possibly help us clear Doc." She regarded me with a startled expression. Was it because I asked a stupid question or because I was willing to help her?

"I guess so." She sniffed and dabbed her eyes. "Maybe Doc won't be so mad if I have someone on my side. I hope as mothers, you'll understand why I did what I did." The tears stopped and her face relaxed. She was ready to get this off her shoulders.

"Let's go find Doc. We'll explain what happened. He seems like an understanding guy."

"Oh, he's been so good to me," she said. "I hope he doesn't fire me. I need this job." We walked back to the entrance of the museum. She stopped and looked me in the eye. "My ex-husband laughed and told me I'd never be able to survive without him. He insisted I'd eventually crawl back to him." Marianne had a far-away gaze in her eyes as if she relived the moment.

My heart ached for her. Fear overwhelmed me when I went through my own divorce. Wade never said those same words to me, but he left me financially broke. I experienced first-hand the distress of having to support myself. I could relate to Marianne's distress.

By the time we made our way back to the lobby, Doc had returned and was talking with Dee Dee.

"Hi, Doc. Any news?"

His face held the answer. "No. Nothing new." He looked as forlorn as a little boy who wasn't old enough to go hunting with his daddy.

I nudged Marianne. It was now or never. "Doc, Marianne needs to talk to you. I think we'd better go somewhere private."

We all traipsed behind the counter and into Doc's office. Penny had returned with Doc, so she volunteered to man the front desk.

"Doc, I realize you're going to be mad at me when I reveal what I've done," Marianne said. "I'll probably lose my job."

"Why don't you let me be the judge of that?" Doc took Marianne's hands in his own.

I was touched with the display of compassion. I wondered how compassionate he'd be when he found out what Marianne had to say.

"I'm so sorry for what I've done. I know better than to do something dishonest, but I was in a tight spot and couldn't figure out a solution." Marianne's chin quivered and she dropped her head.

"Go ahead dear. It can't be that bad." Doc's gentle encouragement seemed to give her confidence to continue.

"I needed money. After my divorce I had to start over on my own. I didn't have a job." Her eyes pleaded for empathy. "I couldn't let my daughter go hungry, so I borrowed as much money from the bank as possible." She looked at me. I nodded.

"Well, that doesn't seem so bad," Dee Dee said. "I borrow money all the time."

"No, I guess it wouldn't be that bad. But, I was in way over my head and felt like I was drowning. When I received the bookkeeping job at the museum, the temptation was more than I could handle. I took a little money from the register every now and then." By this time the tears flowed. Doc let go of her hands and sat back in his chair. He couldn't have appeared more surprised if Gloria Hamilton had patted him on the back and congratulated him on a job well done.

CHAPTER TWENTY

"P lease don't inform the police," Marianne choked out between sobs. "I fully intended to put the money back. But, one day Jacob saw me take some from the cash bag. Next thing I knew, he made unwanted advances toward me. I said I'd report him, and he told me to go ahead – he'd tell you I took the money."

"So you didn't say anything?" I couldn't imagine how terrified she must have been. Her actions put her in a lose-lose situation. She'd made a bad decision at the time when she'd been left to raise her child alone, and now it had come back to haunt her. If Mama hadn't offered me a place to live, I don't know what I'd have done. But I wondered if this young woman could have been panicked enough to kill Jacob. Although there were moments I'd hated Wade, never enough to murder.

"I'm so ashamed." She hid her face in her hands.

"Uh, I'm shocked." Doc slid his chair back, stood up and walked around the room. With hands behind his back, he paced for a few minutes then sat back down.

"I don't have a notion how to handle this." Doc gazed at the top of Marianne's head. "Marianne, why don't you take the rest of the day off? I'm not saying I'm going to fire you, I just need time to think."

The tears flowed faster. Dee Dee handed Marianne a fresh Kleenex. She blew her nose in a most unladylike honk.

Marianne turned pleading eyes up toward Doc. "I'm aware I did something wrong, but I'm asking you to please put yourself in my shoes. I'm willing to pay back all the money. I'm sorry, please forgive me."

I thought of how many times I needed the forgiveness of others. Through experience, I also understood how hard it was to forgive sometimes. The whole scenario brought back painful memories. Wade had dropped the news, out of the blue, he wanted to end our marriage. He'd found his soul mate online, a beautiful, blonde, twenty-something. My world turned upside down, and he left me to pick up the pieces.

They say what goes around comes around. In Wade's case, the saying came true. His beautiful blonde soul mate was in reality a 300 pound bimbo who played men for what she could get. By then, it was too late to preserve the marriage. Wade wanted out.

The anger and bitterness began to eat away at me. It wasn't until Dee Dee helped me see that if I continued to harbor these feelings they would destroy me. God had a good plan when he asked us to forgive others. When we forgive someone who has hurt us, forgiveness can heal that hurt. Even though I'd made progress in forgiving Wade, every now and again I still thought of him as 'the jerk.' *Lord, please forgive me.*

"Trixie." Dee Dee brought me out of my reverie. "Marianne just left. What were you thinking about, anyway?" She squeezed my shoulder. "Wade?"

I'm not sure if it's a curse or a blessing to have a friend who knows you so well. "I don't want to talk about it." I swiped at a tear that ran down my cheek. "I don't think we can accomplish anything else here. Why don't we go pick up Nana and go to lunch. I'm starved."

"Let's go!" She grabbed her signature style gigantean purse faster than Nana could spot a good-looking guy.

Doc sat at the table with his head down. "Look Doc, it's obvious you have a lot of information to digest," I said. "We'll leave you alone while you decide what you want to do about Marianne."

He raised his head and stared at us like he'd just realized we were still in the room. "I can't believe it. She's such a sweet girl. I didn't need this problem on top of everything else." He stared into his empty coffee cup. "I think I'll take some quiet time to pray about this situation. The Lord knows I need all the help I can get."

I hated being the bearer of more bad news, but a thought entered my mind. "You're aware, if Jacob threatened Marianne, it's possible she killed him to get out from under his control."

Doc's head shot up. "No!" he said. "I can't believe she'd hurt another human being. She may have stolen some money, but she wouldn't kill anyone."

He was extremely upset, and I didn't want to cause him further stress. But Marianne definitely gained a place of honor on our suspect list.

We said our good-byes and walked out into the humid air. On our way to the parking lot we crossed the abandoned railroad tracks. Several historic train cars rested on the tracks, in front of the museum, reminiscent of a time gone by.

"Oh, fiddle-dee-dee," Dee Dee said.

"Why are you talking like Scarlett?"

"I saw the Gone with the Wind Museum. I just couldn't help myself." We both laughed.

"All right, Scarlett. What were you fiddle-dee-deeing about?"

"I forgot to ask Doc where Susan Gray works. She's next on our list of suspects."

"Why don't you call him on your cell phone while we drive to the hospital to pick up Nana?"

The visitor's center next door was a hive of busy tourists. After we crossed the tracks, I turned and looked at the three story, red brick building. If I had a chance tonight, I'd read the book Dee Dee found in the antique store. I wanted to learn more about the family who once called this home.

CHAPTER TWENTY-ONE

W hat did Doc say?"

Dee Dee flipped her phone closed. "He said Susan owns Magnolia Books and Antiques, the bookstore where I found the Andrews' Raiders book. We probably met her while we shopped." She replaced her phone in her purse.

"We can go by the shop after lunch and talk to her."

"Well...."

"Well what?" I asked. "Does that 'well' have something to do with your conversation with Doc?"

"Yes. He invited us to come to a ball they're hosting tonight. The history museum is sponsoring a Civil War period gala, and he thinks it will be a good place to meet some of the people on our list."

"What? One, nobody gives balls anymore and two, where are we going to find dresses with hoop skirts?"

"Doc has it all figured out. He said the Gone with the Wind Museum is renting gowns for tonight. It's late notice, but I think it'd be fun and we can do some sleuthing while we're there." Dee Dee pulled down the vanity mirror. Maybe she pictured herself as the next Scarlett O'Hara.

"That's a great idea. But when will I ever get any work done? Harv's gonna' kill me if I don't touch base with him shortly. Remind me to call him later."

"Okay. If you remind me to remind you." She slapped her leg and guffawed. I just grinned.

We pulled into the hospital parking lot and went in to fetch Nana. This time, we maneuvered the corridors like experts. Like all hospitals, the unappealing smell of antiseptics lingered in the air.

We walked through hallways where pictures of employees of the month hung. Portraits of past directors adorned another wall. My mind had traveled a million miles away when I opened the door to Dora's room. Someone practically fell on top of me. I gazed into the gorgeous eyes of Dr. Rossi.

"Oh, I'm sorry," he said.

"No, I'm sorry," I sputtered. "I wasn't paying attention."

With a sweeping gesture he motioned for us to enter the room. He was a gentleman as well as a hunk. What a combination. I experienced a guilty twinge, as thoughts of Beau popped into my mind. But, I guess it doesn't hurt to look.

"Don't worry. No problem. If I had to fall on top of someone I'm glad it was you." He stared straight into my eyes and grinned. Was he flirting?

"Uh..." I was speechless. Leave it up to Nana to fill the void.

"Well, I agree with you Dr. Rossi."

Oh my goodness. What was I going to do with her?

"Nana!" I felt the heat travel from my neck to my cheeks. I realized I was probably tomato red. Being easily embarrassed had always been a problem for me. Never able to hide my feelings, I felt exposed to the world at times.

I glanced at Dee Dee for help. She stood with her hand over her mouth. Was that a laugh she stifled? I'd make her pay for being a traitor.

"Well, you ladies have a nice visit. The patient is coming along nicely and should be able to go home soon." With that he left. He probably couldn't get away from matchmaker Nana quick enough.

"Nannna! What am I going to do with you?" I wanted to throttle her, but hugged her instead.

"Ah, you love me anyway." She hugged back.

I held her at arm's length and looked her over good. "You got that right!"

Even though I loved Nana with all my heart, I understood how Mama became so frustrated at times. When my mother was young, her parents died and her mother's sister, Nana, raised her.

After Nana's husband died she went into a deep depression. Mama stepped in and insisted Nana move in with her.

Nana recovered nicely, but her strong will grated on Mama's nerves at times. I was glad she remained at home to enjoy the peace and quiet. Now I was responsible for Nana's care until we returned to Vans Valley. Thinking about Mama brought tears to my eyes. I owed her so much for her support over the past few years.

When Wade forced us into a financial nightmare we lost everything, including our house. When I didn't know where I was going to live, Mama let me stay in her garage apartment. Suddenly, I felt a tremendous urge to call her.

"Ladies, if you don't mind, I'm going to the visitor's lounge to make some calls." I reached in my purse for my phone.

"Sure. I'll keep the girls company," Dee Dee said. "And don't forget to call Harv."

Ugh, I'd forgotten, but that was probably because I didn't really want to talk to him. Work was the last thing on my mind.

"Oh, I meant to tell you, Nana. We came to pick you up for lunch. When I get through with my phone call we'll go to this place I noticed on the way over. It's called Kountry Kousins and boasts the best home cooking around."

I no sooner reached the end of the hall when my phone rang. I almost jumped out of my skin.

"Hello."

"Hi, sweetie."

"Mama. You are not going to believe this, but I was about to phone you. I had this gut feeling I needed to call. Is everything all right at home? Is Bouncer giving you any trouble?"

"No, dear. Your dog is fine. Everything is fine. I just wanted to check on you." I could picture her sitting in her favorite recliner, feet up, as she talked. "Has Nana driven you crazy yet?"

"She's playing matchmaker with me and Dora's doctor. I have to admit he's handsome, but I'm not interested," I insisted. "Well maybe just a little."

The melodious sound of Mama's laughter floated through the phone, touching that homesick spot I hadn't realized was there.

TWENTY-TWO

Beau's very lonely," Mama said, making me wish I was there with all of them. "He's dropped around the past couple of days. I know he'll be glad when you return. If you're not home soon he might just come and get you."

"I miss him, too. Beau could help us with this murder case if he was in Marietta."

"Trixie, are you involved, again?" I felt like a child who'd been caught sneaking a cookie.

"I can't very well leave, now we've gotten Dora involved. I promise I'll be careful."

"I don't want you to get mixed up in a murder investigation like you did in Dahlonega," she said. "It's too dangerous. I'm beginning to wonder if this journalism job leads you down a path of trouble."

I made a choking sound. "Of course it's not dangerous. It's just a coincidence."

"A coincidence you've been in the vicinity of two murders. I'm not so sure."

"I'll be careful." I fully intended to keep that promise.

"I talked with Jill and she's coming to Marietta tomorrow for a school project and wants to meet up with you." Jill, my only child, is a student at the University of Georgia.

In mid-sentence with Mama, I spotted Nana flying down the hall. Well, as fast a *mature* woman could run.

"Come on girl. You gonna jabber all day?" She beckoned with her hands.

"It's mom," I mouthed, waving her off.

"Tell your mama good-bye and let's hit the road."

"Mama, did you hear? Nana's anxious to get lunch."

'Hi, Betty Jo,' Nana hollered.

"Well, you go on. We don't want to keep Nana waiting. And above all else please don't do anything stupid?"

Who me?

When we got back to Dora's room, a crumpled suit blocked the door. That suit could only belong to one person.

"What are you doing here Detective Bowerman?" It sounded terser than I expected when it came out of my mouth, but I was surprised to see him. And a little nervous.

"Hello, Ms. Montgomery." At least he wasn't chewing on a nasty cigar this time. "Dora's an old family friend and I came by to say 'Hi' and ask her some questions about the break in."

"Detective, I'm glad you stopped by. Is it true Doc's a suspect in Jacob Wallace's murder?" The room was small, and the smell of stale smoke filled my nostrils.

"Doc told us you took him in for questioning," Dee Dee said. "I've been falsely accused of a murder myself. I know how law enforcement can jump to conclusions." She straightened Dora's covers and fluffed her pillow.

"That's right, Detective." Nana offered her opinion. "I'm proud to say if it wasn't for Trixie and me, Dee Dee would be in the slammer right now." Way to go Nana. Open mouth and stick in foot. Quiet filled the room until the Detective spoke.

"And who told you Doc was a suspect? And we do not call them suspects anymore; we refer to them as persons of interest." He measured his next words carefully. "Ms. Montgomery. I don't care how much you helped on the case in Dahlonega, but you *will not* get involved in this case." He hiked up his pants over his protruding belly. "Do you understand?"

All eyes turned to me. "Yes. I hear you." I wanted to point out I wasn't the one who mentioned getting involved. Every time Dee Dee and Nana were around Detective Bowerman they had to expound on my attributes as a crime solver. I'm sure they meant well, but their bragging kept getting me in trouble.

"Excuse us, Detective, we were just leaving."

We made sure Dora was settled in and comfortable before we left. Detective Bowerman followed us into the hall.

"Ladies, I don't think I need to remind you someone broke into Dora's house. Just keep that in mind and stay out of this investigation." He gave us a firm look, and hustled down the hall.

"Well, shoot, we were just trying to help him," Nana said.

"It's as plain as his rumpled suit Nana, he doesn't want our help."

"Hey, there's Nurse Patton, too bad we don't have time to stay around and pester her." Nana laughed mischievously.

"Nana!" I surveyed the hallway to see if anyone heard her. I have to admit though; I thought it might be fun, too.

"Maybe she'll be here next time," Dee Dee rubbed her hands together.

"Girls, we're awful. Come on let's find some food."

The drive to the restaurant should have taken fifteen or twenty minutes, but we hit a modern day traffic jam from all the tourists.

As I drove, the day turned from sunny to cloudy in a matter of minutes. I could smell the rain before it started. Raindrops drizzled down the windshield, and I hit the wiper button. Nana and Dee Dee talked about Dora's therapy. I used this time to ponder the events of the past few days. What a mess we'd fallen into.

Not only had I offered to help Doc, I had an article due soon. Harv expected a manuscript on the Marietta History Museum and the resident ghosts when I returned home. I needed to focus on work more.

Dee Dee disrupted my thoughts. "Is that it?"

"Yep." I whipped into the parking lot. Only a few spaces remained. A good sign.

"Didn't they misspell Country Cousins?"

"It's catchier this way, Nana. Come on, y'all. Let's check this place out." Dee Dee had the door open before I came to a complete stop.

The building, a log cabin, was a little bit of nostalgia in the middle of suburbia. As we entered, I noticed old timey signs hanging on the walls. Antiques decorated every corner of the quaint restaurant. The hostess, all of 5'2" and a good 150-160 pounds, showed us to a table in the back corner.

"Hello girls. My name is Velma. How y'all doin' today?"

Dee Dee shot her a sad look with her puppy dog eyes. "Well Velma, we're doing pretty well, considering we're starving."

"Shoot, I guess you've come to the right place. Let me tell you about our special of the day." She took a pencil from behind her ear and licked the end. Yuck. She poised it over her pad. "Today we got meatloaf and two vegetables for $4.95. Of course, that includes dessert. Ruth, my cousin and the cook, whipped up a batch of her special bread pudding this morning." Velma rattled off more specials without as much as a pause.

"The meatloaf!" three voices told Velma in unison. While we waited on our food, she brought us sweet tea served in quart jars, a slice of lemon hooked on the rim.

Ice clinking back into her tea glass, Dee Dee smacked her lips. "That's the ticket. Trixie, we should go over to the Gone with the Wind Museum after we finish eating and pick out our dresses if we're going to the ball tonight."

Nana jumped on this like a flea on a dog. "What ball are you talking about?"

Oh boy, Dee Dee let the cat out of the bag. There was no way out of this but to tell Nana about the fundraiser.

"The Marietta History Museum is giving a Civil War period gala tonight, and Doc wants us to attend so we can meet some of the Board members. The Gone with the Wind Museum is graciously providing dresses for attendees." I took a refreshing sip of cold, sweet tea. "Why don't you spend the night with Dora while we go to the ball?"

She stared at me like I'd grown two heads. "Are you crazy?" She scrunched up her face. "You *are not* going to leave me out of this. You know, me and Scarlett have a lot in common." She clapped her hands. "Oh, this is so exciting."

CHAPTER TWENTY-THREE

Velma muttered as she approached our table. "I told her so, but nooo she wouldn't listen." She shook her head. "Girls, sorry to have to tell you this, but we're out of meatloaf." We issued a collective groan.

"Ruth never takes my advice. She's Ms. Know It All. I told her she didn't make enough meatloaf. It's always a crowd pleaser, so it wouldn't hurt to have more than enough. But no, she doesn't want to have too many left overs," Velma spouted. She put her hands on her hips and took a determined stance.

"That's all right Velma," Dee Dee tried to cut her off before she continued her tirade. "What choices do you have available?"

"Let me think." She flicked her pencil on her chin. "We have plenty of steak and gravy or fried chicken. I'll let you have either one for the same price of $4.95."

I chose the steak and gravy. Dee Dee and Nana went for the fried chicken. Cholesterol heaven here we come.

We talked about Dora's progress and then discussed who we'd question next. "Let's go to the bookstore first thing in the morning and talk with Susan. Dee Dee, you can look around and I'll find some reason to ask her questions."

While we planned, Velma and a young lady brought our food to the table. Good grief, each plate held enough food to feed a starving family of five.

"Did I hear y'all mention Susan over at the Magnolia Books and

Antiques down on the square?" Velma wiped her hands on her apron, and struck a pose.

"Do you know her?" Dee Dee asked.

"Yep. She comes in here now and again. She always treats me like I'm some second-class citizen. Sure, she has money and is dressed in them nice clothes, but that don't make her any better than the rest of us. She puts her pants on the same as we do. Anyway, I've heard she's about to lose her antique store."

She glanced over her shoulder to see if anyone was listening and leaned in conspiratorially. "As a matter of fact, I've seen her and Jacob Wallace in here more than once. Lookin' all goo-goo eyed at each other."

Susan and Jacob as a couple was definitely an interesting twist. This information could take the investigation in a different direction. "Really? Are you sure?"

"Of course I'm sure. I've lived here all my life and know most everyone from around here. A good number of people who work down on the square eat here." She looked at me indignantly.

"That's good news, Trix. Maybe she killed Jacob and we can get Doc off the detective's hit list."

"Yeah, ain't that great, Trixie," Nana said.

I kicked Dee Dee's shin under the table, I wasn't sure if Velma would tell Susan about our snooping. I had to put a sock in Nana and Dee Dee's mouths.

"Ouch, what did you do that for?"

"Oh, I'm sorry. It was an accident."

"Sure it was." Dee Dee reached under the table and rubbed her ankle.

"Thank you, Velma. We'll holler if we need anything else." I hoped she'd take the hint and leave.

"Hmph. I'll be back to check on ya." She turned on her heels and left us to our delightful bounty. We bowed our heads and said a little prayer of thanks. I dug into my food like I'd never eat again. The helpings didn't look so big after all.

We enjoyed silence the next few minutes while we wolfed down our chow. Ruth's home cooking was some of the best I'd ever eaten in a res-taurant. No wonder they ran out of meatloaf.

I laid the crumpled napkin on the table and patted my stomach. "Ladies, I feel like a stuffed turkey on Thanksgiving morning."

"Me, too," Dee Dee agreed.

"Well, I didn't have much of an appetite after all." Nana's plate sat empty on the table. I'd hate to see her when she was hungry.

"Ladies, y'all ready for your check?" Velma laid the ticket face down on the Formica. "I don't know what you want to speak to that ole' Susan Gray about, but I'm sure she and that Wallace fellow was up to no good."

I was sure they were, too. "Thank you, Velma. And you tell Ruth the food was to die for." Oops, maybe not the best choice of words.

"Yes, me too," Nana said. "Some of the best vittles I've ever eaten."

"Well, y'all come back now. Ya hear?" Velma laughed and slapped her leg.

It was a little after two in the afternoon, so we headed over to the Gone with the Wind Museum. We could go pick out our dresses, and then have enough time to go back to Dora's and take a quick nap.

Before Dee Dee could reapply her lipstick, we pulled onto the his-toric Marietta Square once again. Now familiar, with all of the trips we'd made downtown, the rain had stopped and the sun shone bright as a hundred watt light bulb. The air smelled fresh, and several tourists had already ventured out, enjoying the cooler air in the park, located in the middle of the square. Some window shopped as they walked along the sidewalks.

We parked and made our way over the railroad tracks. Nana kept up like a trooper. She talked a mile a minute about being Scarlett.

"Oh, I can't wait to get my dress," Nana said. "I'll look just like Scarlett. You wait and see."

"Well. I rather fancied myself being Scarlett." Dee Dee patted her head with the palm of her hand as if patting her curls.

"Okay, girls. Let's not get into a cat-fight. You can both be Scarlett. Once the ladies put on their dresses for the evening, all of them will probably feel a little like Scarlett." I had to admit, I was getting excited. I've always wanted to dress up in a beautiful ball-gown.

We walked into the Gone with the Wind Museum. The building appeared deserted at first. "Hello, may I help you?" An attractive, middle-aged lady greeted us.

"Yes. We want to rent gowns for the museum fund-raiser they're having tonight." Her eyebrows rose to her widow's peak.

"Oh, my. You've come at a most inopportune time. The dresses have been picked over, but we may have something left." She motioned for us to follow her through the hallway and back into a side room. "I'm afraid this is all we have. I'll try my best to fit you with something."

I picked up a velvet, maroon dress I thought would fit me. I ran my fingers over the soft material.

"By the way, I'm Susan Gray. I volunteer at the museum and I'm helping out today. We've had a last minute run on dresses." Her gaze swept over all of us. "You'd think people wouldn't wait to the last minute."

I literally dropped the dress I held. "Oh, I'm so sorry. Did you say your name was Susan Gray? Do you own the Magnolia Books and Antiques Store?"

"Yes, I do. How did you know?" The tone of her voice reflected her wariness.

"Uh, Doc. Doc Pennington told us you're on the board of the history museum." I picked the dress up from the floor. I wanted to try it on. "I'm Trixie Montgomery and I write for "Georgia by the Way".

"Yes, I'm familiar with the magazine. We have some copies in the bookstore."

"This is my friend and assistant, Dee Dee Lamont." I'd called her my assistant so often; I'd begun to believe it. I placed my hand on Nana's shoulder. "This is my great aunt, we just call her Nana."

"Well, we need to get you ladies fitted if you plan to attend tonight." She pulled out several dresses and held them up to Nana. Most of them would swallow her whole. She told us to wait and after a few minutes she returned with a sure-fire replica of Scarlett's gown. Nana's eyes lit up like a ten-carat diamond.

"We've just received this dress. The mayor's wife was going to wear it, but she changed her mind. I see no reason why we can't use it. She handed the dress to Nana. "Would you like to try this on, ma'am?" What a silly question. I don't believe Sherman's troops could've stopped Nana. She grabbed the dress from Susan's hands quicker than a dog on a biscuit.

Now, for Dee Dee. After several more attempts we found one Dee Dee liked. I wasn't sure it would zip up, but I wasn't going to bring it to her attention.

"Dee Dee, why don't you go help Nana, and I'll wait here?" I wanted to question Susan alone.

Dee Dee didn't take the hint. "Oh, come on. It'll be fun if we all try them on at the same time," she suggested.

I winked at Dee Dee, trying to grab her attention.

"Trix, is something in your eye?" Dee Dee asked. "You do seem to have a problem with that. Maybe you need to get your eyes checked."

"Let me see. I'll get it out." Ever helpful Nana got right up in my face. I feared she would stick her finger in my eye and try to pluck out what wasn't there. I popped up over Nana's head and glared at Dee Dee.

"Please take Nana with you and I'll follow in a minute." She finally took the hint and off they went to try on their outfits.

"Susan, do you mind if I ask you a few questions for an article I'm working on about the Marietta History Museum?"

She jumped at the chance to share her expertise. I asked a few benign questions at first and she answered them willingly. Then I loaded for bear. "Susan, is it true you had an affair with Jacob Wallace?"

"Who are you, and what do you really want?" Susan's eyes bore straight through me.

CHAPTER TWENTY-FOUR

L ook. I've been working on an article for the history museum and we were in the museum when they found Jacob's body. Doc's been implicated in the murder, and I'm trying to help him." I had no idea how long Dee Dee and Nana would be gone. I hurried to get as much information as I could before they returned.

"Velma, over at Kountry Kousins, told us you and Jacob met at the restaurant several times. I'm trying to understand why you'd meet someone you insisted Doc fire for making unwanted passes at you. Did you make that up?"

"No. I didn't make it up." She never took her eyes from mine. "And it's none of your business."

"I have a suspicion of what happened."

"Then why don't you tell me?"

I'll give it my best try. "This is what I believe transpired. I believe Jacob did make passes at you. But rumor has it Jacob's a nice looking man and possesses a way with the ladies. I think he charmed you into having an affair." I hesitated, studying her reaction. Her wide eyes and "O" shaped mouth indicated I'd hit pretty close to the truth. I continued.

"In the meantime, you'd fallen in love with Jeffrey, who'd asked you to marry him. The choice was easy. A wealthy man over a handyman any day. You couldn't let Jeffrey find out about Jacob, who had threatened to tell Jeffrey, so you cried wolf. Am I warm yet?"

"I don't know what you think gives you the right to come in here and accuse me of anything. Even if you are on the right track, and I'm saying *if,* what would my having an affair with Jacob do with the murder?" Her shoulders dropped and her eyes narrowed, darting around the room.

"Maybe you wanted to shut him up. If he had threatened to tell Jeffrey the truth, it would certainly be motive enough to kill him." Boy, I couldn't keep my mouth shut. I was worse than Nana and Dee Dee.

She grabbed the dress out of my hands. "If you want to try this on then I suggest you do it now. You've worn out your welcome. And take those two biddies with you."

Looking back, I'm surprised I made it out of there alive. I wouldn't appreciate a stranger prying into my business. But, to get answers I had to ask questions.

Our dresses didn't fit perfect, except for Nana's. It fit like a glove. I admit Nana made a cute Scarlett O'Hara. Dee Dee and I would have to make do with ours.

"Y'all are not going to believe what Susan called you." I couldn't resist the temptation to pick at them.

"What?" Nana asked.

"She called you 'biddies.'" I made sure to put an emphasis on biddies.

"Who is she calling an old biddy?" I thought I saw smoke swirl from Nana's ears. Dee Dee quickly caught on I was toying with them. We laughed until I had tears rolling down my eyes.

"What's so funny? You wouldn't laugh if she called you a biddy." She turned toward me from the passenger seat.

"Oh, Nana. Don't get all riled up. I was just trying to lighten the mood. She was mad because I asked her some hard questions. You won't believe what I discovered."

A distinctive click alerted me Dee Dee had released her seat belt. She leaned up toward the front seat. "Well, give us a try," she said.

"Actually, I guessed most of it, but her reaction confirmed I was on the right track. Jacob made passes at her, just like she said. But, after a while, she fell under his spell and they had an affair. At the same time she'd been dating Jeffrey. He asked her to marry him. There was no way she was going to give up the chance to marry money. Especially since her store was in jeopardy of being foreclosed on." I stopped to get a breath. A chorus responded from "really?" to "wow!"

"By this time she was desperate, she didn't want Jeffrey to find out about the affair, so she told everyone Jacob made passes at her. She insisted Doc fire Jacob to shove him out of the way."

We pulled into Dora's driveway. I turned toward Dee Dee. "What do y'all think? Did she kill Jacob to keep the affair from Jeffrey?"

"I've heard of people killing for less. Just watch that television show '48 Hours.' People kill for the most bizarre reasons," Dee Dee said.

"That's right." Nana held on to her Scarlett dress with a death-grip. "I've seen that show and those people are plum crazy. I'd say she's definitely a suspect."

"Well, come on. Let's go in the house and figure out what shoes we're going to wear with these get-ups, then take a long nap. I, for one, am getting too old for all this running around." Dee Dee handed me the two dresses in the back. I leaned into the car and bumped my knee. Pain shot through my leg. I longed for a good long soak in that claw-footed tub, but knew that was out of the question.

"Speak for yourself, Trixie. I'm ready for the nightlife. Bring it on." I just love my Nana. But I knew I would need God's help to make it through this evening with her in tow. *"Lord, please give me the strength and patience to keep up with Nana."*

I don't know how long I'd been asleep when I heard the doorbell. I struggled awake, slipped on a robe and answered the door.

"Hello, Ms. Montgomery." Detective Bowerman pushed his way into the house. "Did I wake you?"

"Yes, sir. You did." *What does he want now?* "May I help you?"

"Msss. Montgomery." He drew out my name for emphasis. "I thought I told you to stay out of this investigation." He hiked up his pants. Either they were too big for him or he'd acquired an ugly habit.

"I don't have any idea what you're talking about." I crossed my fingers behind my back.

"I think you do," he said. "Susan Gray called me and she's not happy. Actually, irate would be a better description. She said you asked her personal questions as well as questions related to the case. She claimed you harassed her. I explicitly told you to keep your nose out of this. What part of that did you not understand?" By that time Nana and Dee Dee were standing in the background, listening to the detective's tirade.

"Detective. I am a journalist and it's what I do. I ask questions. I was doing my job, gleaning information from a board member of the history museum." Well, it's the truth. I do have to ask questions for my job.

"That's right, detective," Nana spoke up. "She was just doing her job. And we were there on official business. I'm Scarlett."

"Beg pardon, ma'am." The detective gaped at Nana.

"Just what she said. She's Scarlett. We're going to the museum fundraiser tonight and we went to the Gone with the Wind Museum to borrow our dresses. In no way did we harass her."

Nana had scooted out of the room and came back in holding up her dress.

"See?" She positioned the dress in front of her and twirled around. I hoped she didn't fall over from dizziness.

"Oh, I see." A slight smile crept across his face, then faded.

"Well, I don't want to tell you again, Ms. Montgomery. And that goes for you two ladies, as well." He gave Dee Dee and Nana a scathing look. Like that would deter them. "This is serious business and you could get hurt. I'd feel mighty bad if you were harmed on my watch." This time he looked at me. "Do you understand?"

"Yes, sir." I understood perfectly well, but I didn't promise him anything. He stuck his cigar in his mouth and took leave. The tobacco aroma lingered in the air after his departure. I much preferred the smell of sweet honeysuckle, which was in full bloom outside Dora's window.

"Okay. Let's grab a quick sandwich and get dressed. It'll be time to leave shortly," I said.

"Scarlett. May I help you with your dress?" Dee Dee used an exaggerated southern accent to address Nana. I had to laugh at their antics. Maybe it would be fun.

If we'd only known what the night held, we'd have stayed home and played checkers.

CHAPTER TWENTY-FIVE

Nana looked precious in her dress. The moss green velvet overskirt with a chartreuse underskirt had a gold belt, imitating the drapery cords. It resembled the movie's costume, right down to the little green hat perched on Nana's head. There might be more than one Scarlett tonight, but none would be as cute as Nana.

Outside, the air was laden with a sweet summer fragrance from the gardenia bushes Dora had planted. Further down the walkway near the carport, honeysuckle and magnolia vied for my senses as we made our way to the car. What a fitting night for a ball.

When we reached my Jeep, I realized I'd given no thought to how we we'd fit three hoop skirts inside. Nana and I held Dee Dee's dress while she attempted to climb into the back seat. After a couple of failed attempts, I placed my hands on Dee Dee's behind and pushed for all I was worth. She shot forward.

"What did you do that for, Trixie? You almost killed me."

"I didn't mean to push so hard."

"I bet you didn't. You sure that wasn't payback for something I did?" She gathered the voluminous dress and spread it around her.

"Of course not. Come on Nana, you're next." It wasn't quite as hard to get Nana settled. She's a lot smaller than Dee Dee, so I didn't have to heave as much. I carefully arranged her dress. She grinned from ear to ear.

By the time I positioned myself behind the wheel, I was exhausted. I said a little prayer for my Jeep to start. Usually hit and miss, I'd threatened more than once to get a new car. The thought of a big payment kept me from making it happen. Now I'd passed the six month probation period on my job, it might be a good time to buy one. If I could get the story written and turned in, I reminded myself. I turned the key and let out a sigh of relief when the motor cranked.

"Tara, here we come." Laughter reverberated throughout the car.

"Trixie, do you think the murderer will be at the ball tonight?" Dee Dee's skirt swished as she repositioned it.

"I don't know, but we should stick close together just in case. You can never predict what a desperate person might do."

"Well, I want to find me a man. And this will certainly be the place to do it. Rhett Butler has to be around here somewhere and I aim to find him." Nana said in her best Scarlett voice. She took her fan from her reticule and fanned herself. I didn't know if it was for show or because she thought about Rhett. I'd have to keep my eye on her.

As we approached the country club, cars lined both sides of the road. "Wow, look at the crowd. We'll never find a place to park." I frantically scoured my surroundings for a space.

"Look! They have valet parking." Dee Dee thrust her arm beside my face to make her point. She barely missed my nose.

A young valet, who scarcely gave us time to disembark, jumped in my Jeep and drove away. We stood behind several people waiting to enter. I noticed the attendees handed cards to the gentleman at the front door. Panic struck as I realized they were invitations.

I poked Dee Dee. "Look, they have invitations. Did Doc mention invitations?"

She poked me back. "No. He didn't. What are we going to do?" We were next in line.

"Hi ladies." The doorman gazed at Nana and smiled. "Ms. Scarlett, how are you tonight?"

"Just fine thank you," Nana answered.

A mountain of a man, with baseball mitt sized hands, shoved a palm toward us. "Could I see your invitations, please?"

"Uh, yeah. You could if we had any. Doc Pennington invited us, but he didn't say we needed an invitation."

Dee Dee nodded her head in agreement.

"Sorry ladies. I'd love to let you in, but I can't without that piece of paper."

I panicked. My lungs tightened and my cheeks warmed with embarrassment. Here we were, standing around dressed like Scarlett wannabes without a way in the party.

Everyone gave us questioning stares as they moved passed us, presenting their embossed invitations. Dee Dee pushed me out of the way.

"Look, just go find Doc Pennington. He'll vouch for us." She no sooner had the words out of her mouth than the man himself walked up.

"Hi, Jerry. These ladies are friends of mine and are here at my invitation, please let them through." Doc looked at Nana. "And who is this charming young lady? I don't think we've met." Nana actually batted her eyes at him.

"Why, I'm Scarlett, of course," she said without missing a beat. *Oh, puleease.* Nana and Dee Dee were taking this way too seriously.

"This is my great-aunt, but everyone calls her Nana."

He kissed her gloved hand. "Well, it's a pleasure to meet you, ma'am. Why don't you ladies follow me and we'll go and find Penny. She'll be so glad to see you." We gathered up our skirts and dutifully followed.

The room glowed, ablaze with color. The ladies were dressed in the most beautiful array of hues: green, blue, yellow, red, and every color in between. The men wore fine pants and coats with many of them wearing period military uniforms. Music filled the air and swirled around the room. A young man danced and sashayed his partner from one end of the dance floor to the other, keeping in time with the Blue Danube.

I noticed Penny, standing alone, across the room. She stood by the refreshment table kneading her hands. Face pinched, she didn't look any more relaxed than the first time I'd met her. I suppose I wouldn't be either, if my husband was a suspect in a murder case. We zigzagged through the maze of partygoers to where she stood.

"Oh, Trixie and Dee Dee. I'm so happy to see y'all. Doc told me you're helping him clear his name." She grabbed ahold of Doc's arm like she'd never let go. "I'm so grateful to you both." She turned toward Nana. "And this must be Scarlett O'Hara." Nana grinned like the Cheshire Cat.

Doc pried Penny's death grip loose and pulled me aside. "Is there anyone in particular you haven't met on your suspect list I could introduce you to?"

"I haven't met Jeffrey yet, or Gloria Hamilton's son." I glanced over my shoulder to see if anyone might be listening.

"Right. He seems like a nice kid. Gloria's pushing for him to have my position. He'll be here tonight."

"Ladies and gentlemen, may I have your attention?" As if on cue, Gloria was standing at the podium. "Thank you all for coming tonight. Rest assured this fund raiser is for a great cause. Let me give a little background on the Marietta History Museum for those of you who are not familiar with its history.

"The building that houses the Marietta History Museum was built in 1845 as a cotton warehouse. Dix and Louisa Fletcher, from up North, purchased it in 1855, remodeled, and opened it as the Fletcher House Hotel.

"During the early years of the war, the hotel was used as a Confederate hospital and morgue. In addition, Andrews' Raiders stayed in a second floor room on the evening prior to their theft of the steam engine, "The General."

A smattering of oh's and ah's filtered through the rapt crowd.

"The Union Army eventually requisitioned it, and when General Sherman came through town on his "March to the Sea," Fletcher House did not burn down, however, the roof did catch fire from cinders blown over from nearby buildings, and the fourth floor was never rebuilt."

I looked around to see if a young man who looked like Gloria might be watching his mother's speech, but no one jumped out at me as her son.

"After repairs were completed in 1867," Gloria continued, "Dix Fletcher reopened the hotel, and renamed it the Kennesaw House. It remained a hotel until the 1920's, when the first floor was converted to retail shops, leaving the hotel on the second and third floors.

"In 1979, the building was converted to an office complex. It would be 14 years until the building was turned into the Marietta History Museum, and has remained much as you see it still today. As you can tell, it behooves all of us for future generations, to keep this building with such a rich history, financially sound."

A round of polite applause agreed with Gloria's appeal.

She held out a hand. "I would like to take this time to thank the Board for all of their hard work. Let's also give them a big round of applause."

The history of the museum would greatly enhance my article, but not once did she mention Doc or Penny for their time and effort given to the museum, and her pointed glare at him drove home my suspicion. This lady obviously had it in for Doc.

CHAPTER TWENTY-SIX

Now, everyone, please enjoy the rest of the evening." Gloria stepped down from the podium. Nodding acknowledgements, she headed straight for our little group. "Well, hello Doc. Penny. I see you've brought some guests with you tonight. I don't remember them on the invitation list."

"I invited them," Doc bowed low, his confederate general's suit made him especially dapper. "Trixie is doing everything she can to help us with publicity for the museum."

"Yes. I've met Trixie." She spewed my name like it was a disease. "She claims to work for "Georgia by the Way." And who might these ladies be?" Her gaze lingered on Dee Dee and Nana, raking them over from head to toe.

"I introduced you to my friend Dee Dee this afternoon, and this is my great-aunt Nana."

"That's Scarlett to you, Missy." Oh great, just what I needed in front of *the* Gloria Hamilton. Nana acting like she believed she was Scarlett. Then I noticed Gloria's dress. It was very similar to Nana's except it was purple velvet with a lavender underskirt. The strange color reminded me of grape Kool-Aid. With the magic of the night, maybe all the ladies believed they were Scarlett.

I didn't exactly picture myself as Scarlett, but I did feel pretty. I wished Beau could see me. Feeling pretty didn't happen often for me. Low self-esteem is something all women struggle with at times. The models on television and magazines have made it impossible for *normal* women to meet unreal standards. I try to remember that the fantasy world of television celebrities doesn't represent normal. God loves what is on the inside much more than what's on the outside. I stood a bit taller in my period costume.

A handsome young man walked our way. Gloria raced over and grabbed him by the arm to pull him toward us. I suspected he was in his late twenties. Tall and lean, he made a dashing figure in his Rhett-like suit. He possessed a chiseled face and light brown hair, more of an Ashley Wilkes. You could swim in his blue eyes, and he boasted the longest eyelashes of any man I'd ever seen. If this was Gloria's son, no wonder she was so proud of him.

"Ladies, I'd like you to meet my son, Steven." Gloria brushed a piece of lint from his jacket, hovering around him like he was a young child.

"I hear you recently graduated." Dee Dee gave him a dazzling smile.

"Yes, ma'am. I received my Doctorate from the University of Georgia."

Wow, smart as well as handsome. No wonder Gloria was vying for him to take over Doc's position. That still didn't make it right. She had no call to push Doc out of his post. It couldn't be that long before he retired.

Nana surprised me with her next words. "Sir, would you like to dance?" Oh my goodness. What was she up to?

Steven answered without missing a beat. "Why, I'd love to Scarlett." Nana grinned from ear to ear as she hooked her hand though his crooked elbow. They made their way to the dance floor.

We sipped on lime punch as we discussed the museum's history. In a few minutes, Sammy, whom I met earlier at the museum, asked *me* onto the floor for a lively polka. *Why not?* I jumped at the chance to pry some information out of him.

"May I call you Trixie?" Sammy bent over in a gentlemanly bow. Once on the floor he was a wonderful dancer.

My knee ached, but I toughed it out. I didn't want to miss this chance. "Oops, didn't mean to step on your foot." *Way to go, Trix.*

"A little lady like you can't hurt my foot. Don't worry about it." Regardless of his denials, I sensed he pulled back a little.

"Sammy, what keeps you busy when you aren't attending board meetings?"

"I own a real estate company. Most of the buildings in downtown Marietta are part of my holdings."

A smug grin appeared. He acted the exact opposite of Gloria's son Steven. Where Steven appeared humble, Sammy exuded arrogance. I suppose if you owned most of a town the power might go to your head.

As I was pondering the differences between the two men, without warning, the lights went out. Everything happened so fast. Pushed from behind with forceful hands, I fell to my knees. Screams split the air. Then I realized the shrieking was mine. As quick as the lights went out, they came back on. The entire episode lasted only a matter of minutes.

I lay on the floor writhing in pain. I grabbed my knee. *Lord, please help me.* Someone called for an ambulance, and then everything went black again.

Dee Dee's round face hovered an inch above me. We both emitted a little screech.

"Well, it's about time you woke up." She grabbed my hand and gave it a squeeze.

"Yeah, you had us worried to death." Nana pushed Dee Dee aside to peer down at me. They were still dressed in their Scarlett dresses. I didn't care if I never saw a hoop dress again in my lifetime.

"Somebody knocked me down when the lights went out." I knew it was no accident. Who wanted to hurt me? Were we getting too close to the killer?

"Guess who your doctor is?" Nana cooed.

"Nana, please. I don't feel like guessing." My head throbbed and my knee ached.

"You don't have to. Here he comes." Dee Dee moved out of the way.

Dr. Rossi loomed over me, his white coat almost as bright as his pearly whites.

"How is our patient feeling?" He leaned over and looked into my eyes.

Well a little better now that you're here.

"I fell on my bad knee. The pain caused me to black out." I surveyed the area. The curtained off area and the voices close by tipped me off we were in the emergency room. "Do I have to stay overnight?"

"No, not if you promise to prop up your leg and stay off that knee as much as possible for several days." He tapped his pencil against the chart. "We've taken x-rays, and nothing's broken. Have you been told you are going to need a knee replacement soon?"

"Yes. I've tried to put it off as long as possible. I don't know how much longer I can hold out." I raised my head to garner a look. Yuck, it was swollen and had already turned blue and purple.

"I promise to keep off it tonight." Well, that was better than no promise at all.

"Doctor Rossi, you release her into my custody and *I'll* promise she won't go anywhere." Nana winked at me, then the Doctor. "You make house calls?"

While I wished I could disappear altogether, he seemed unaffected.

"I'm sure you'll look after her." Doctor Rossi laid his muscular arm across Nana's thin shoulder.

"I'll get the nurse to wrap you, and I want you to go home and ice it. Keep it propped up as much as possible. You need to visit an orthopedic surgeon when you return to your home town." He drew back the sheet, and gingerly felt around on my sore knee one more time.

I flinched.

"I'm sorry if I hurt you." His touch reminded me of Beau, and how much I missed him. Even though we'd only been dating a few months, I realized how much I loved how he made me feel safe when I snuggled in his arms. I needed him.

"Ladies, I'll probably see you again when you visit Dora. Please take care, and call my office if there's anything I can do for you." A nurse drew the curtain back and informed Dr. Rossi another patient needed his attention "STAT."

When he'd left, the emergency room nurse deftly wrapped my knee while Dee Dee drove the Jeep to the patient loading area. I dreaded not being able to drive for a few days.

An attendant wheeled me out through the emergency entrance. Dee Dee helped me in the car. Still dressed in a hospital gown, I detected a cool breeze blow from behind. I grabbed for the back and pulled the pieces together. I had no desire to show my rear end to the world. Nana had to sit in the back this time. Dee Dee had her hands full helping her in. Even through the pain, I couldn't help but smile at Nana as she sat in the back seat with her dress spread around her.

Silence shrouded the car. For a few minutes anyway. "Trixie, what's going on? Are you positive someone pushed you down? Are you sure you didn't fall."

"I'm sure I didn't fall. I felt hands push hard on my back. Someone purposely wanted to hurt me." I mentally pictured the suspects who were at the ball. It couldn't have been, Sammy, he was in front of me. I flashed back to being in his arms one minute and on the floor the next.

Nana leaned forward. "Who would want to hurt you, Trixie?"

"I'm not sure who, but I think I know why. Someone doesn't appreciate me asking questions. I must be getting too close to the killer."

CHAPTER TWENTY-SEVEN

Right now, I want to get home and lay my weary body down." I prayed the pain pills would kick in soon and result in a good night's sleep.

"Yeah, me too," Nana said. "But didn't we have an exciting night? I'm so glad I didn't miss out on this one." I rolled my eyes and hoped Nana wouldn't notice in the dark.

Rhett and Scarlett were sitting in the library, when I heard the phone ring. That's strange; they didn't have phones back then. *Oh, it's my phone.* I glanced at the clock. Morning had arrived way too soon, and I'd been dreaming of Tara.

"Hello." I managed to squeak out.

"Hi, Mom."

"Jill? How are you doing, sweetie." No matter how old she became she would still be my sweetie. Yes, we've had our disagreements as parent and child have during the teenage years, but she had grown into a mature young woman.

"The question is, *how are you doing*? Dee Dee called me last night and said you took a pretty awful spill and wound up in the emergency room. Did you hurt your bad knee?"

"Yes I did. But don't worry. They wrapped it and instructed me to keep my leg propped up as much as possible." I patted the bulky bandage. "I brought my cane."

"Do you feel well enough to meet me for lunch? You can bring Dee Dee and Nana, too."

"Of course, I do. I'll ask them, I'm sure they'll jump at the chance to eat lunch out."

"There's a pizza place on the square. Would that be okay with you?" Not my favorite food, but I knew she loved pizza, so I acquiesced.

"That's fine. How about one o'clock? Maybe the lunch rush will be returning to their jobs?" I wasn't in the mood for a crowded pizza joint.

"It's Papa's Pizza. And Mama, I have a surprise for you." She sounded so excited. I couldn't imagine what she had for me. Maybe it was a late birthday present.

"Can't wait to see what you have for me." We said our good-byes and I decided to go ahead and get up. I could smell bacon frying; I knew Nana was up cooking breakfast. I attempted to sit up, but searing pain shot through my knee. I'd need to take it a lot slower than I'd thought.

A multi-colored knee greeted me as I unwound the bandage. My joint showed decreased swelling since it had been propped up all night, but not enough to drive. Dee Dee didn't yet have an inkling she'd just volunteered to be my chauffeur. I hobbled into the kitchen.

Nana, decked out in a jogging suit, stood at the stove holding a spatula. Dee Dee already up, was dressed in Capri's and tee shirt. "Hey, ladies." Thank goodness they weren't in their Scarlett dresses.

"Good morning, Trixie." Dee Dee and Nana spoke in unison. Dee Dee stuck a pancake laden fork in her mouth. She wiped excess syrup off her chin.

"How's that knee? You look a little green around the gills."

"The last time I felt this bad was when I gave birth." Speaking about birth jogged a memory. "Hey, did y'all hear what Wynonna Judd said about giving birth?" They shook their heads. "She said having a baby was like trying to pass a ham through your nose." The snorting sounds emitted from three women were not pretty. The laughter relieved some of the built up tension we'd experienced over the past few days.

"Come on, Trixie. Sit down and grab a plateful of these pancakes," Nana said. "You need all the strength you can get." She stacked five pancakes on my plate. Granted, they weren't huge, but they weren't little either. *Oh, what the heck.*

"We've already offered the blessing, so dig in." I couldn't get the fork to my mouth quick enough.

"Okay, Missy." Nana grabbed my plate almost before I was finished. "You go right back to bed. Dr. Rossi said you should rest your knee." Nana balked at being bossed, but she didn't mind being bossy.

"That's right." Dee Dee agreed.

"Sorry. Bedrest ain't gonna happen today. There's work to do. My article isn't finished, and I'm still helping Doc. We're getting close. First, Dora's house was broken into and then someone pushed me down?" Today I'd planned to visit the Marietta National Cemetery. Over 10,000 union soldiers laid to rest in this historic landmark. This would be great material for my article. "And I'm meeting Jill for lunch."

"I can't make you stay in bed, but why don't I drive you around today?" Dee Dee must have read my mind.

"I'll take you up on that offer." I rubbed my aching knee. "Jill said she has a surprise for me. Want to come see your grand-niece, Nana?"

"No, dear. If you don't mind I think I'll go sit with Dora. Would you give Jill my love?" I exhaled when she declined the invitation. I don't know how Mama did it, keeping up with Nana everyday. She harbored more energy than a two year old.

I hobbled back to my room and dressed the best I could with my swollen joint. Khaki Capri's with a blue short sleeve tee would have to suffice. Nana, as usual, had dressed sharp as a tack. She sported a watermelon colored running suit with a white short sleeve shirt underneath. Jogging co-ordinates were her favorite outfits: spring, summer, winter or fall. And they always had to match. I admit she looked spiffy.

Dee Dee had chosen denim Capri's. She had on a multi-colored, and I do mean multi-colored, pull-over blouse. On her wrists she wore a myriad of colorful bracelets. Bright pink Keds adorned her feet. I loved Dee Dee's fashion flare. Her colorful outfits never failed to bring a smile to my face. I needed to have a serious meeting with the clothes in my closet and brighten up my wardrobe.

We released Nana at the main entrance of the hospital. I couldn't visit Dora, but I was sure she'd understand when Nana explained.

"Where to, James?" Dee Dee guffawed. "I've always wanted to say that."

"I think that's *home James*," I said.

"Whatever, it's still fun to say either way."

"We've talked with everyone on the list but Jeffrey. Let's find him and see if we can question him before we meet up with Jill?" A warm glow filled me with the thought of seeing my daughter. It'd been too long.

"Sounds good." Dee Dee latched onto the wheel with both hands and took a corner like she sat in the driver's seat of a race car.

I grabbed the handle above the window. "Whoa. Slow down, you're going to get us killed, or run over some little old lady."

"Aw, you're just jumpy this morning. I wasn't going that fast. You relax, and leave the driving to little ole' me." Relaxing while she drove was an oxymoron.

"Let me see your list and I'll check where Jeffrey works." I thought he worked at one of the banks, but I wasn't sure which one.

"It's in my purse." She scooted it toward me. Dee Dee's love for large bags was no different today. She had a hot pink purse to match her shoes. It sported a giant pink flower on the front. I removed a billfold, brush, bottle of Tums, and an address book before I found the tablet.

"Hmmm, you've written down the First Trust Bank located a couple of blocks from the square. I think I've seen it going to the hospital. Take a left at the next...." She took the corner so fast my heart palpitated, and I feared it would fly out of my chest. "Good grief, Dee."

"Well, you said take the next left." She slowed behind a truck loaded with hay bales. "Out of the way, Farmer Brown!"

I silently offered a prayer of thanks when we managed to arrive without running down any little old ladies or kids. I couldn't wait until I could drive again, because Dee Dee would certainly be the death of me.

CHAPTER TWENTY-EIGHT

T here's a parking place right in front." Since I couldn't walk far, I was grateful for a space this close.

"Allll righty!" She parallel parked quicker than a lizard hiding under a rock. I was impressed.

It appeared like any other bank – ostentatious. I would never understand why banks built such enormous buildings. The bank is located on the bottom floor and who knows what is on the other levels.

The receptionist hung up the phone as we arrived. "May I help you?"

"Yes. Could you tell us where Jeffrey Jones' office is located?"

"Sure. Go down the hallway, and his office is the last door on the left." She turned around and returned to her business.

Raised voices filled the hallway as we walked toward the office. And they weren't friendly. I lifted my hand to knock on the door when I overheard a familiar voice. "Just remember what I said." Sammy turned around and saw us standing in the doorway. "Excuse me ladies." He took off like a fox chased by hound dogs. *What was that all about?*

"May I help you?" Jeffrey sat behind an oversized mahogany desk. Framed certificates covered the dark paneled wall. "Weren't you at the museum fundraiser the other night?" He stood up, and looked directly at me. "I believe you're the one they transported in an ambulance."

"That's right." Not knowing if he was one of the bad guys, I didn't want to give away too much information. "I have a bum knee and I fell when the lights went out."

"I hope it's better." He looked at my cane, motioning to two red leather visitor chairs in front of his desk. "Now what can I do for you?"

"I'm Trixie Montgomery and I write for "Georgia by the Way." I motioned toward Dee Dee, who had made herself comfortable, and I sat in her chair's twin.

"I'm familiar with "Georgia by the Way." He leaned forward and settled his hands on his desk. "What does that have to do with me?"

"I'm working on a story about the museum. The night Jacob was killed, Dee Dee and I were there."

He stood up, walked around his desk and closed the door. I wondered what he had to hide. I intended to find out.

"I'm interviewing all the board members. Can you tell me a little about your position at the museum?"

I let him drone on about his love of history and the antiques he'd collected over the years. It was time to get to the nitty-gritty.

"Jeffrey. Doc is in a lot of trouble. Detective Bowerman, the investigating officer, has his sights on Doc. We're trying to help him. Did you demand Doc fire Jacob for making passes at Susan Gray?"

"Yes, I did. And I don't see why you're getting mixed up in this." He leaned forward, arms crossed. "What is it to you?"

"Trixie helped solve a murder last year in Dahlonega, and saved my hide." Dee Dee told him. "She's got a knack for it. When Doc found out he was in deep, he asked Trixie to help."

I couldn't tell who owned the biggest mouth, Dee Dee or Nana. *It's a toss-up.*

"Really?" He stared directly into my eyes. I didn't like the way he glared at me. Fear gnawed at the pit of my stomach, and perspiration beaded on my forehead.

"And what have you found out so far?" He glanced from me to Dee Dee.

"Well, let's see," Dee Dee began. I faked a pneumatic cough hoping Dee Dee would put a lock on her lips. She grabbed the water from Jeffrey's desk and handed it to me.

"Drink it, Trixie. It'll keep you from choking." When I didn't take the water she shoved it in my hands. "Drink it! I promise it will work." I was going to *choke her* if she didn't sit down in her chair.

"I'm all right now." We had to make a quick escape. The hair on the back of my neck stood up. I was getting a real bad feeling about Jeffrey. "Come on, Dee Dee. I think I need to go, I'm not doing well."

Jeffrey opened the door for us. "I'm sorry you're not feeling well, Ms. Montgomery. Please be careful. Digging into a murder investigation could turn out to be dangerous." Was it my imagination or did he over emphasize "danger?" Relief flooded through me as we exited the building.

Back in the car Dee asked, "Where to James?" This time, her joke fell flat. She wasn't as perky as earlier, and neither was I.

"Let's head to the museum and see if Doc's in. Maybe he can update us on his status with the detective."

"Trixie, what if Doc killed Jacob? We don't know him that well. Maybe we're wasting our time."

She had a point. But my gut told me Doc was innocent. I prayed my gut wasn't wrong. Our lives depended on it.

We pulled into the parking lot. I grabbed Dee Dee's arm before she could exit the car and gave her my serious look. "Don't you dare pretend you're Scarlett. I've had enough of Scarlett for the rest of my life."

"Okey dokey, your wish is my command. Obviously your knee hurts and it's making you grumpy."

I was grumpy, and my knee did hurt, but I couldn't give up. We were close. Maybe too close and someone tried to stop us.

Marianne manned the front desk. "Hi, I'm glad to see you."

"I'm glad to be here." Marianne met my gaze, her eyes clear and bright. "Doc and I worked out a plan so I can repay what I took."

I patted her hand. "That's wonderful. Is he in?"

At that moment, Doc walked out of his office and saw us. "Hey, there." He eyed my cane and gently took my elbow. "Penny and I were so worried about you. Come in and sit down, tell me how you're doing." He led us into his office.

"I've been better. The question is how are you doing?" He showed me to a chair and waited until I settled in.

"Not so good," he said. "Detective Bowerman has been back, questioning me several times. He's relentless. Maybe he thinks I'll confess if he wears me down. If so, he's in for a big disappointment. I'm not going to confess to something I didn't do."

"Doc, Trixie and I believe we're getting close. That's why Dora's house was broken into and Trixie was pushed down last night," Dee Dee said.

"I appreciate your help, ladies. But I don't want you in harm's way. You probably shouldn't try to investigate anymore. The case is getting too dangerous." He shook his head and his shoulders drooped.

"We're already in up to our eyeballs. The killer doesn't want us to finish what we started, but we don't have a choice," I argued. "It's imperative we find out who the killer is before he kills us." I readjusted my bottom on the seat. The worn chair had lost its padding long ago.

"We've interviewed all the people on our list: Marianne, Susan, Gloria, Jeffrey, Sammy and Steven. Each and everyone have a motive. Jacob was blackmailing Marianne. By the way Doc, we're happy to see Marianne still here."

"I gave it a tremendous amount of thought and prayer. Jesus had a lot to say about forgiveness. He tells us in Ephesians to "be kind and compassionate to one another, forgiving each other, just as in Christ, God forgave you." He cupped his hands over his face as if he was praying. He was silent for a minute, Dee Dee and I waited.

"How could I not forgive her?" he said. "I've fallen short so many times in my life. Several people have given me a second chance, and that's why I've come as far as I have. I could be rotting in jail in the Bahamas. Penny is going to take over the finances for the museum and I've come up with a plan for Marianne to pay back what she *borrowed*. I pray I'm doing the right thing."

"You're being more than generous and I'm sure she appreciates it," Dee Dee said.

"Not to mention that Gloria is telling everyone you stole the money," I said. "Won't the board demand her dismissal?"

"I have the last word on employees, and Marianne will stay as long as I have a job."

"Then all the more reason we need to find the killer." I leaned back, the chair squeaking in protest. "Let's get back to our list."

Dee Dee pulled a rumpled piece of paper from her bag.

"Susan also has motive," I began. "She had an affair with Jacob and she didn't want Jeffrey to know. On top of that, her bookstore is about to face foreclosure." I mentally put a check by her name. My vote went to Susan. She had the most to lose or gain, depending on how you looked at it.

Dee Dee spoke up. "We visited Jeffrey this morning. When we arrived, Sammy was in his office and we heard them arguing. I haven't figured out what Sammy's motive might be. Jeffrey could have found out about Jacob and wanted him out of the way." She tapped Jeffrey's name on her list to accentuate his guilt.

"That leaves Gloria and Steven," Doc stated. "I can't envision Gloria being strong enough to kill anyone, and I'm not sure she has a motive. I know she wants Steven to take over as director, but killing Jacob wouldn't guarantee Steven's appointment." He pushed his glasses up on his nose and wiped his brow with his handkerchief.

"That's not exactly true, Doc," I said. "If you go to prison for killing Jacob, then Steven could step in as director with her recommendation. So she does have motive."

"Put that way, I guess you're right," he said.

"That goes for Steven as well. It would be to his advantage if you were out of the way, Doc." I thought back to last night, when I met Steven. He seemed like such a nice young gentleman. I struggled picturing him as a killer.

"We need to go, Trixie. It's time to meet Jill." Dee Dee pointed to her pink watch.

"Doc, we're meeting my daughter for lunch, but if you think of anything else please let us know."

"I will. But please, please be careful." Famous last words.

TWENTY-NINE

"I'm starved. Where is this Papa's Pizza?" Dee Dee scanned the roadside, hands on the wheel.

"It's on the next corner. I hope you can locate a parking place close to the door. If not, then let me out front." We weren't successful finding a space close enough, so Dee Dee dropped me off and left to park the car. I was anxious to see Jill.

She ran up and rewarded me with a big hug, and I hugged her tightly.

She stepped back and inspected me from head to toe. "How are you feeling? You're using your cane again."

"I'll be fine. I'm scheduled to visit the surgeon when I get home." My goodness, she looked great. Her presence was the best medicine I could receive.

When her father and I divorced, I worried how the separation would affect Jill. My fear she'd choose sides, was unwarranted. She's been supportive of me and I've tried to be supportive of her when she wanted to talk about Wade. After all, he's still her dad.

"Come on over and sit down. I want to show you my surprise." I couldn't wait to see what she'd brought. *A guy?* What in the world was she doing with a guy? Well, never mind, I know what she was doing with him, but she never mentioned her surprise was a date.

"Mama, this is Paul. Paul this is my mother." Standing, he towered over me by at least six inches. We shook hands. He pulled the chair out for me to sit down. No wonder she couldn't wait for me to meet him.

I winked at Jill. Her face turned a pretty shade of pink and her smile widened.

"Where are Nana and Dee Dee?"

"Nana sends her love. She's sitting with her friend Dora today. And Dee Dee's parking the car." Just then she walked in, and I gave her a big wave. "Over here, Dee Dee."

We repeated introductions and I could see Dee Dee was enamored with Paul, too. We ordered pizza all the way around and pigged out until we couldn't hold any more. I updated Jill on my article, but failed to mention anything about our part in investigating the murder. I didn't want her to worry.

"Mama, it's been so good to see you. But, we have to return to Athens today, so we need to be on our way." She reached over and laid her hand on Paul's. I could tell this was serious. I hoped she'd fill in the details later. They stood up to go, Paul grabbed the check, insisting on paying for the meal. "Let the cops do their job, this time, Mama." Jill gave me a hug, and then Dee Dee. "Dee Dee, watch after her." How ironic. Dee Dee was usually the one who got me into trouble in the first place.

"I promise to be careful if you do as well, honey, those roads can be—"

"Mama. I love you!"

We walked them to the door. Saying goodbye was bittersweet. I waited on Dee Dee to retrieve the car. When she returned, I attempted to get in as fast as I could, but it wasn't easy with a swollen knee. An impatient person blew their horn. Dee Dee, decked out in her pink Keds, got out and stomped back to the car. The woman in the little red Mini Cooper shrunk down in her seat. Dee Dee went up to her window and said something to her. The lady nodded her head yes. Dee Dee climbed back in the Jeep.

"What was that all about?" I really didn't need to ask. I knew full well she probably gave the poor woman a lesson on disabilities.

"Oh, she needed a little educating." She put the car in gear and pulled off, followed by the Mini Cooper.

"You ready to go to Dora's and rest?"

"Yes. But there's one more place I need to go. I want to take some pictures of the Marietta National Cemetery for my article. It's located on Washington Avenue, the road that leads into town." All articles for the magazine required accompanying photographs. I'd neglected my research, so it was imperative to concentrate on my journalism for a bit. This would be a great opportunity to accomplish some work.

"Hang on. Here we go!" Dee Dee sped down the road out of town and toward the historic cemetery. We arrived in a matter of minutes. "Wow, look at that archway. Isn't it beautiful?"

"From what I've read, it's one of five archways that lead into a National Cemetery." I glanced in my side mirror. Someone in a red over-sized truck pulled in behind us. "Dee Dee, there's a truck behind us. Let's park away from it so I don't get it in my pictures."

"I would, but he's following us. Every time I make a turn, he turns, too."

"Pull over here and maybe he'll go around us." I turned around to see if he was going to pass. Instead the passenger jumped out wearing a ski mask. In this weather?

"Get out!" He shouted. His hand was in his pocket as if he had a gun pointed at us, so we obliged. "Hurry up and give me that book."

"I don't know what you're talking about," Dee Dee said. "What book?"

He gestured wildly with his pocket. "Yeah you do. The book you bought downtown."

A truck rumbled by on the road, but trees blocked the driver's view of us, hands in the air.

"I know you have that book written by the union soldier. And you'd better hand it over quick. I don't have time for your shenanigans."

"Oh, I think I know what book you're talking about now. It's in my purse." Dee Dee walked back toward the Jeep.

"Don't do anything funny. I've got you covered." He followed Dee Dee as close as he could while she reached in and retrieved her purse. He grabbed it from her and rummaged through the contents. "Good grief, lady. What do you have in this suitcase?"

"Don't ruin it. It's one of my favorites, and it matches my shoes." Only Dee Dee could worry about her bag while being held up.

He raised the book and declared, "I knew it." He threw the purse at Dee Dee's feet. "Do not follow us or you'll be sorry." More pocket brandishing, and he turned and ran. He hopped in and they sped away. I memorized the first three letters on the license plate before the truck sped past the arch.

"What in the world was that all about, Trixie. It's just an old book. Why would they want it?"

"Do you think it has something to do with that diary, do you suppose they thought we had a copy?"

"Well, we're going downtown right now and telling Detective Bowerman what happened. This hit too close to home. All of these events can't be coincidental. They have to be connected to the murder investigation." This is one time I couldn't agree more with Dee Dee.

"Come on. I can take pictures later." I was concerned Dee Dee would have a heart attack before we arrived. Not from fear, but from anger. She was so mad someone stole her book and her dignity in the process.

A young lady sat soldier straight behind the front desk of the police station. She wore a crisp uniform, her hair pulled back in a bun. "May I help you?"

"Yes," Dee Dee said. "We've been robbed."

"Really?" She reached for a tablet to take notes. "What did they steal?"

Straight-faced Dee Dee said, "a book."

"Oh." The officer didn't appear to be as interested when she found out it was a book. I think I saw a smirk on her lips. "Have a seat." She pointed to a row of dirty, orange seats lined against the wall.

"Yuck! I don't want to sit in those," Dee Dee whispered.

"Me neither, no telling what we might catch. They look like they're covered in cooties."

I turned back to the officer. "Would you please inform Detective Bowerman we're waiting? This might concern a case he's working on."

She looked at us like, 'yeah sure.' "What are your names?"

"Just tell him Trixie Montgomery and Dee Dee Lamont need to see him as soon as possible."

She picked up a phone, and punched a button. I wondered if she'd tell him, or pretend to and send us on our way. I couldn't blame her. Who in their right mind would report a stolen book?

CHAPTER THIRTY

Hello, Ms. Montgomery. Ms. Lamont. What can I do for you, I'm very busy?" He wasn't wearing a jacket today, but Bowerman's shirt was as rumpled as usual. I didn't spot his cigar. He looked kind of naked without it.

"We've been robbed," Dee Dee exclaimed.

"So I've heard." He hiked up his pants. "Come on in my office." He sounded reluctant, but motioned us to follow him down a hallway into a dingy cove filled with the scent of male – stale cigar smoke and sweat. The interior decorator had gone for early utilitarian. A large desk pitted with numerous dings and scars sat center stage. No pictures adorned the wall. Two ragged chairs sat in front of the desk. On the desktop sat a picture of a middle-aged woman with two teen-aged children. I was taken aback, I'd never pictured the detective with a family.

"Your family, detective?" He actually smiled, revealing smoke stained teeth.

"Yes, ma'am." He turned the conversation back to the reason for our visit. "What's this about a book robbery?" He unwrapped a cigar and stuck the pacifier in his mouth.

"We went to the National Cemetery to take pictures for my article. Some strange man jumped out of a truck and ran up to us. He insisted we give him the book."

"Could you describe this book?" The detective removed his cigar and twirled it between his fingers.

"I bought it at the Magnolia Books and Antiques Store downtown,"

Dee Dee said. "A Union soldier, one of Andrews' Raiders, wrote the book. I don't understand why the robber wanted it."

"For some reason he wanted this book bad enough to hold us at gunpoint." Dee Dee scooted to the edge of her chair and put her elbows on the detective's desk. "And would you believe he threw my favorite purse on the ground?"

His caterpillar eyebrows crawled up. "Did you get a good look at the assailant?"

"He wore a ski mask, detective," I told him. "He sped away in his truck, but I memorized the first three letters from the tag – PAT. The truck was red and had one of those oversized diesel engines with the double tires on back. I think they're called duelies."

"Did he hurt either one of you? Threaten you?"

"He brandished a gun." Dee Dee announced.

"What kind of gun?" Now we had his interest. He moved several stacks of paper from one side of his desk to the other. He scrounged around until a pen hovered over a notepad. "Tall? Thin? Did you recognize him?"

We told him everything we could recall, and he took copious notes. When we couldn't remember any more details, he looked up. "You never said if it was a pistol, shotgun?"

I glanced at Dee Dee. "We didn't exactly see the gun."

Dee Dee held up her hand, finger pointed like a gun barrel. "Kept it in his pocket."

Bowerman's chair groaned as he leaned back. "Never saw a weapon." He tossed his pen down. "I suppose you were smart to believe it was a gun. Ladies, with all due respect, I'm too busy to spend any time tracking down a book robber." He stood up, stogie motioning to the door. "And I'm sure this has been stressful for you." He hurriedly escorted us to the door. "I'll call you if we learn anything. The results from the crime scene at Dora's should be in shortly."

We left him shaking his head, and I doubted he'd take any action at all. For all intents and purposes, our book thief did not have anything to do with Doc's troubles.

"Come on, Dee Dee. I need to go home and prop up my leg. I'm exhausted and my knee is killing me."

"It's about time you decided to take care of yourself. I'll get you to Dora's as soon as I can."

All I wanted was to go home and see Mama and Beau. I missed them so much. First, I had to finish this article and leave the investigation to the professionals. We were getting close and it scared me.

We stopped by the hospital and picked up Nana. When we arrived at our temporary home I propped up my leg and crashed.

"Wake up. Detective Bowerman's on the phone. He wants to speak to you."

I rubbed the sleep from my eyes, and squinted up at Dee Dee holding the receiver under my nose. I grabbed it from her. "Hello? This is Trixie."

"I wanted to inform you we made an arrest in the robbery. Susan Gray master-minded the break in."

"What? Why?" I sat up, my head spinning with the sudden movement, and the astonishing news. Why would she go to such lengths to steal a book?

"The Civil War book Dee Dee bought at her store is a one of a kind. Susan claimed it's a first edition, signed by the author. It's worth a lot of money. She never intended to sell the book in her store. An employee mistakenly placed it with the sales stock. When she found out her assistant sold it to Dee Dee she panicked. Fear of losing the book prompted the break in at Dora's. We have her fingerprints, and Susan admitted she searched Dora's house for the book."

My head reeled, wheels spinning. "Detective, do you think she's connected to the murder?" It would be a great relief if Susan's arrest set Doc free from suspicion.

"I don't see any connection."

"We're not close to making an arrest in the case. But you don't have to worry. I just wanted to call and inform you of Susan's involvement. This should put your mind at ease concerning the break in. Now you take care of your knee and leave the investigating to us."

"Thank you for calling. This definitely makes me feel safer." The click on the other end of the phone did not make me feel any better about Doc.

"What was that all about?" Dee Dee stood so close to me I could smell toothpaste on her breath.

"You're not going to believe this." Nana sashayed in my bedroom dressed in a Victoria's Secret nightie. "Susan Gray was behind the robbery yesterday. She hired those two men to steal the book from you."

"Why in the world did she want an old book?" Nana vied for a place beside me.

"The book is old. It's a signed, first edition and it's extremely valuable. The author was one of the Andrews' Raiders. She wanted to sell to the highest bidder to bolster finances for the bookstore. The detective said she's the one who broke into Dora's the other night. I can't believe she was so desperate."

"Well, that's a relief," Dee Dee said. "Come on, girls. Let's get dressed and ride into town for a big breakfast. We deserve a little pampering."

Nana gingerly sat down so as not to jostle. "Trixie, how are you doing today? Is your knee any better?"

"It's sore, but better than yesterday. I can't wait to get home and see the orthopedic surgeon." *Did I really just say that?*

"Well, take your time getting ready, and we'll go have a humdinger of a breakfast."

An hour later we pulled onto the road. Though my knee was better, I still wasn't up to driving. I'd have to endure another day of Dee Dee's racecar antics. We voted unanimously to eat at Kountry Kousins. Velma seated us and took our orders.

"I'll have eggs, grits, bacon, toast, and coffee." Nana said. How did Nana eat like a dog with worms and never gain an ounce.

"You want to share with me?" I asked.

"No, I don't. You can get your own." She unwrapped her utensils and floated her napkin into her lap.

"In that case, I'll take the same thing she's having." They say a hearty breakfast starts your day off right.

"Just make that three, Velma," Dee Dee said.

"What do y'all think about Susan being the killer? She's got my vote." Dee Dee spread strawberry jam on her toast.

"I'm not so sure she's involved. Robbery is one thing; murder is a whole different ballgame. I'm not counting her out though. As we've said before, people will kill for the most insignificant reasons." I grabbed my fork and scraped my plate, foregoing etiquette. Hands down, this had to be the best breakfast I'd ever tasted.

"Ahhh, a good breakfast, the case is almost solved and while I rested last night I came up with a hook for the article. Things are really going well, except for the old knee."

CHAPTER THIRTY-ONE

et's head over to the museum and tell Doc the news about Susan. This could be the break we've been looking for." Dee Dee reached for her pink flowered purse and withdrew her new lipstick, Pink Pansies. She swiped her lips and pursed them together. Her pink lips matched her pink outfit. I smiled.

"You girls go on out to the car," Nana said. "I need to visit the little girl's room. I'll meet you outside in a few minutes."

We paid our bill and stepped into the bright sunshine. I looked forward to having a productive day.

"Look how this van parked," I observed. "They didn't have to park so close."

"Yeah, crazy drivers. Let me help you in."

Dee Dee came around to my side to assist me. The door on the white van next to us flew open and a man jumped out and grabbed me. Another grabbed Dee Dee. Before we could shout for help, someone shoved us rudely into the back of the van. Another man pointed the barrel of a gun at us.

"Jeffrey? What are you doing?" Dee Dee asked incredulously. "Where are you and Sammy taking us?"

"You'll find out soon enough. Now shut up." It seemed like forever, but it could have been a few minutes. Time moved in slow motion.

Dee Dee and I exchanged frightened glances. What would Nana think when she couldn't find us? Were they going to grab her, too? It was all starting to make sense. I knew without a doubt these two men were involved in the murder.

When the van stopped, and the door opened again, we were in an old warehouse, darkened windows kept out any light. A dim glow came from bare light bulbs dangling from the ceiling. The building was empty, save for a few wooden crates scattered here and there. Within minutes we were forced to sit in straight back chairs with our hands tied behind our backs and our legs bound at the ankles. My knee throbbed.

Dee Dee whispered the obvious. "Trixie, I think we found the killers."

"I think you're right."

"Y'all need to keep your traps shut. Your big mouths got you in trouble in the first place." Jeffrey stomped over and tested the ropes wound around our wrists.

"Hey, you didn't have to pull so hard," Dee Dee said. "That hurt."

"It won't make any difference in a little while. Your pain will be irrelevant."

Yikes. I didn't like the sound of that.

"Sammy, why did you kill Jacob?" I thought I knew the answer, but I wanted to keep him talking. Hopefully Nana recognized something terrible had happened and called 911.

"He didn't kill Jacob. I did." A chill ran down my spine; I recognized that voice. I turned my head to confirm my suspicion. There stood Steven.

"Jacob's death was most unfortunate. I never planned on killing anyone." He walked in front of us. He didn't appear so handsome now that I'd discovered he was a murderer.

"Then why did you?"

"Shut up! You don't have to tell them anything." Sammy hadn't said much up until now. I couldn't believe these three successful men had thrown away their futures.

"It's doesn't matter. They won't be able to talk to anyone when we finish with them."

I had to keep them talking. Our lives depended on Nana attaining help in time. "Sammy, I think I've figured out why you and Jeffrey are involved, but I don't understand why Steven would kill Jacob."

"Go ahead and tell us why," Sammy said. "I'd love to hear your theory."

"I haven't put all the puzzle pieces together, but I'll give it a try. Sammy, you told us you owned a majority of the downtown property. I think you wanted the museum for the property it sits on. And since Jeffrey is a loan officer, he planned to give you a loan to buy it."

"She thinks she's pretty smart doesn't she, Sammy?" Jeffrey's sneer filled me with fear.

"Steven, you seemed like such a nice young gentleman. How did you get mixed up with these two?" Dee Dee asked.

"It's your fault." Wasn't it just like a crook to blame someone else? "I was there to scare you off the night you were at the museum. I never intended to kill anyone. When I discovered Jacob at the museum he startled me. I couldn't take a chance on him telling anyone I'd been there." He clinched and unclenched his fist. He resembled a wild animal.

"We were in the Andrews' Room, so I grabbed the gun with the bayonet on it from the display. It all happened so fast. But what's done is done. I can't bring him back." As Steven paced back and forth in front of us, I wondered if he'd be the one to kill us.

Sammy took the floor. "Y'all just had to poke your noses in our business." He looked directly at me. "You insisted on asking questions like you were some kind of cop. If you hadn't shown up, our plan might have worked. We tried to convince the board to sell the museum so I can build some condominiums. With a loan from Jeffrey's bank and our investor we could have made millions."

Jeffrey waved his gun around like a crazy man. "Yeah, women. They're no good, two-timing, low-down scum." I had a feeling he referred to Susan. I thought it sounded more like my ex-husband, Wade. I suppose it all depended on which side of the fence you were on.

I knew it was time for a prayer. *Lord, please protect us and let Nana find help.*

The door burst open and two of the biggest hombre's I'd ever seen charged in. Before I knew what happened, the two mountain men slammed Jeffrey and Sammy on the floor and handcuffed them. Steven escaped.

But not for long. In marched Detective Bowerman, with a small army of police officers. They had Steven in tow. Suddenly the group of officers parted like the Red Sea and Nana walked through.

"Thank God you're all right." She rushed over and kissed my cheek. "I was so afraid we wouldn't make it in time. Girls, meet my friends Mad Dog and Viper." She motioned toward the two burley, tattooed guys who'd come to our rescue.

"Ladies." Bowerman looked toward us. "If it wasn't for your Nana here, we wouldn't have found you. You can thank her for keeping her wits about her." That was too funny. Wait until Mama heard that one.

"Detective, they're behind the murder. Steven's the one who killed Jacob." I suspected I'd be giving a full statement later.

"Oh? How so?" Caterpillar brows shot up.

"How does a full confession sound to you?"

"Mirandize all of 'em!" Bowerman barked.

"Nana, how did you know where we were?" Dee Dee asked.

"When I came out of the little girls room, I saw them push you in the van. Mad Dog and Viper were inside eating. I ran in and told them I needed help. Bless their pea picking hearts. They believed me." She blinked her eyes and shot a smile toward the two men.

Mad Dog pointed his fingers covered with heavy metal rings at Nana. "By the time we ran out to our motorcycles she was already on the back seat. I didn't have time to argue with her about how dangerous it was to ride through traffic chasing a van. We got to the warehouse and called for backup. When we received the word we came in."

They must have noticed the inquiring looks Dee Dee and I wore.

"Take them on out," the detective ordered. Officers escorted the three handcuffed men out of the warehouse, and Bowerman joined us. "Good job guys" He met my questioning look. "Viper and Mad Dog are two of our best men. They're undercover cops. They're on our side. And I believe God must have been on your side today.

"I do, too, detective. I do, too." *Thank you God, for saving our lives.*

A month has passed. I'm sitting here among friends and family. It's my first day home from the hospital. When I returned from Marietta my doctor arranged for knee surgery as soon as possible. I've been staying with Mama and Nana until I can manage stairs.

Detective Bowerman charged Sammy, Jeffrey, and Steven with kidnapping. They spilled their guts in hopes of receiving a deal. Their sentence put them away for a long, long time. And it wouldn't be in condos.

Susan's indictment included breaking and entering as well as robbery. She lost her freedom, as well as her bookstore. The book she desperately wanted became evidence. Doc recovered nicely from the disruption to his life. He decided to give another year to the museum and then retire. Penny couldn't be happier.

There is one person involved in this whole fiasco I felt sorry for. I knew Gloria never expected things to turn out the way they did. She hired Jacob to steal artifacts from the museum, determined to make things look bad for Doc in hopes of having Steven step in as director. Jacob was there that night under Gloria's direction. How ironic that her son killed Jacob.

As for our ghostly visitors that dreadful night at the museum, that mystery remains unsolved. Did they appear to warn us, or were they a figment of highly charged imaginations? We'll probably never know, and I don't think Dee Dee plans on going back to determine the answer.

Harv raved about my story. The best I'd ever written he said. *Where past meets present* is the new motto for "Georgia by the Way." Beau and I have grown closer than ever. When you come through the other side of a life and death situation it's amazing how everything becomes crystal clear about what is really important. Like the people you love. I glanced at Beau.

"I love you."

"I love you, too." He gave me the sweetest kiss I think I've ever tasted. It was a wonderful day to be alive.

QUESTIONS FOR DISCUSSION

- Trixie chose Eph. 4:32 as her favorite verse for "Murder in Marietta, "Be kind and compassionate to one another, forgiving each other, just as in Christ, God forgave you." Do you have a favorite verse? What is it?

- Can you think of an instance where Jesus mentions ghosts in the New Testament?

- Trixie felt obligated to help Doc because he was Harv's friend. In the end she was glad she did and that Doc was found innocent. Have you been in a situation where you felt obligated to help someone, but were glad you did?

- Doc decided to forgive Marianne after thinking about the times others had forgiven him, and remembering the words of Eph. 4:32. Why do we find it so hard to forgive others? What helps you forgive others?

- Gloria Hamilton wanted her son, Steven, to become the director of the Marietta History Museum. Ironically, when she took things into her own hands, she made things worse. Has this happened to you? Have you found it is better to take matters into your own hands or to ask for help from God?

- Trixie and Dee Dee's friendship continues to grow as they encourage each other in their faith. Do you think it's important to have friends who will encourage your faith? If so, why?

- Who was your favorite character? Why?

- What was your favorite scene? Why?